CHUKA ANI

For Adanna and Obinne

Chapter One - Introductions

"Four chocolate biscuits,

a packet of all-butter shortbread,

three packs of crisps,

two chocolate bars

and a couple of cans of cherry cola."

"Cool. That's lunch sorted," thought Chuka, removing his art and music textbooks from his school bag, to make room for all the junk food.

I know what you may be thinking. But no, it isn't this young man's birthday. And it definitely isn't Christmas day. Nor is it 'pay the school bully off with sweets so she'll stop picking on you on sports day *because you're no good at sports*, day'. Or even, 'bribe your teacher with snacks to get better grades because you can never quite seem to concentrate in class day'. This was just an ordinary, plain vanilla, run-of-the-mill-a, not even a big deal-a, 'this is what I *always* have for my lunch' day. How on earth did it end up this way, I hear you say?

Chuka Akunna lived with his big sister - Chinwe, his Mother - Onyeze and Father - Chidozie, in a town called Owerri, in a state called Imo, in a country called Nigeria, in the great continent of Africa. Chuka's family hailed from the Igbo people who are known for their independent nature, creativity and business acumen. The Igbo are just one of the many groups of people in the extremely diverse country of Nigeria. The best way to give you an idea of the vast numbers of different communities living in Nigeria is to avail you of a few interesting facts about the world:

Fact one: There are twenty-four languages native to the *continent* of Europe.

Fact two: The *country* of Nigeria has over five hundred and twenty languages and cultures.

Fact three: The continent of Africa has over two thousand languages and cultures.

Chuka's house, like many homes in hot climates, was painted white to reflect the sun's rays and keep the interior of the house cool. His family were financially comfortable, as was reflected by the house they lived in, which had four bedrooms, a large family parlour, a play room and a large garden. It was situated within a compound that in turn was surrounded by a three-metre wall of bright green breeze-blocks. These hollow walls were home to several local 'red-neck' agama lizards, who spent their days basking in the hot sun, scurrying up and down the wall searching for insects and constantly nodding their heads as if they were warmly saying 'wassup' to their fellow cold-blooded comrades. The garden was lined with dwarf coconut and dwarf palm trees that provided shade on hot, sunny days - which was pretty much every day. Across the road from the house was the local park which Chuka rarely went to, except to secretly salivate over some sugary snack.

Chuka was in his third year at Owerri Secondary School. In his class, he was well known for not doing anything at speed, except for eating. In fact, it had been accurately calculated that his speed was inversely proportional to his greed.

Chinwe, on the other hand, who was in her second year at Owerri University studying Economics, was known for doing everything at speed. Taking after her mother in appearance, she had a short afro, was as sleek as a gazelle and appeared to glide across the ground whenever she ran. She played football, tennis, squash and basketball to name but a few of her many sporting interests. As a result she was always on the go - never staying still for long. Even when she spoke, she seemed to be talking at light-speed.

Chuka's parents ran their own business, buying and selling car parts. His Mum, who was forty-three, was the business brain of the family, having studied Business Management at Owerri University. Even though she was a small, slim built woman, she was a formidable negotiator - always making sure she got the best deal for her business, herself and for her family. However, this no nonsense approach was never applied to her son. Her keen commercial awareness also probably stemmed from the fact that from an early age she had to take responsibility for the finances of herself and her two younger siblings. This was because her parents passed away when she was in her early teens, so she, along with her mother's sister, had to take charge of her family's fortunes. Both her sisters had long since moved abroad to live in Botswana and Rwanda respectively, but she kept in regular contact with them.

Chuka's Dad, who was forty-eight, was the legal expert of the family. He studied Commercial Law, also at Owerri University, where he met his wife. He used his expertise to great effect within the family business, always double-checking, triple-checking and sometimes even quadruple-checking contracts before signing them. "The money is in the minutiae", he would always say as he wiped his glasses, before perusing the particulars. He, like his wife, was also the eldest child with two younger siblings. Both boys in his case. They too had sought their fortunes elsewhere, albeit a bit closer to home, in Lagos state.

Chuka's mum and dad were trilingual, speaking Igbo, Yoruba and English. This helped them do business with several different communities in Nigeria. Chuka and Chinwe spoke Igbo and English. The Akunna family was what you would call 'middle-class', which usually meant that they had more than enough money to buy what they needed and mostly, but not always, enough money to buy what they wanted.

In many ways Chuka was the same as many other thirteen year old boys. He wasn't incredibly smart, but he wasn't dull. He wasn't particularly neat and tidy, but he wasn't a slob. He wasn't very hard-working, but he wasn't bone-idle. He wasn't a 'goody-two-shoes', but he wasn't disrespectful. And he wasn't the most generous boy you'd ever meet, but he wasn't selfish either. Like most thirteen year old boys, he was just a boy in the middle.

What made Chuka different from most other thirteen year old boys is that he completely refused to eat any kind of fruits, nuts or vegetables. He wouldn't eat anything that even *reminded* him of a fruit, nut or vegetable. Not yams, not plantains, not African walnuts, not avocados, not paw-paw (papaya), not watermelon, not bananas, not mangos, not guavas, not odara (star-apple), not pineapple, not oranges, not lemons, not grapefruit, not tangerines, not ube (African pear), not carrots, not coconut, not bitter leaf, not African spinach, not water leaf, not ugu leaf, not African garden egg, not water apples, not cashew nuts, not peanuts, not cassava. Not anything!

From the moment he was weaned, at one year old, he would only eat processed foods like biscuits, and only if they came out of a colourful and shiny packet. As he got older, the theme continued, only eating food that was smothered in something sweet, like tomato ketchup or jam or just plain old, refined white sugar. No one knew why Chuka developed a 'sweet tooth' from such an early age. His father had the curious idea that he only liked to eat sweet things because when Chuka's mother was pregnant with him, she had major cravings for chocolate and ice-cream. She, however, was quick to point out that although she had cravings for sweet foods, she still ate a balanced diet and did regular exercise when she was pregnant with both of her children.

His parents did everything they could to encourage him to eat fruits, nuts and vegetables. They tried to make meal-times fun by cutting them into simple shapes like circles, stars, triangles or half-moons so that they looked a bit like sweets. That didn't work but he did know all his shapes by the time he was four. They tried blending them into smoothies and pouring it into cute little cups. They even tried

freezing the blended fruit to make fruity ice lollies.
But even these cooled concoctions couldn't curtail
Chuka's confectionery consumption.

As you might expect, Chuka's refusal to eat
anything fruity, nutty or veggie had unfortunate
consequences for him. During lunch-time at school,
he would often eat so many of his favourite snacks -
puff puff, (a kind of deep fried donut) that he often
found himself out of breath after just a few minutes of
exercise. This lead to the other children making fun of
him and making up taunts, like: 'you eat too many
puff-puff's, that's why you always 'puff-puff'' and
'you're always eating chocolate cake, and that's what
makes your belly shake.'

Chuka was average height for his age - about five
feet tall. But because of his incessant consumption of
sugary and fatty snacks, he was often last to be
chosen for basketball, football and other outdoor
games with his friends. It got so bad for him that,
eventually, he stopped going outside at lunch-time
altogether. This made things even worse for his
health, because now he wasn't getting *any* exercise,
either at school or at home. Also Chuka's skin didn't

have a lovely milk-chocolaty glow like his sister's because, unlike her, he was not getting the vitamins and minerals he needed from a healthy, balanced diet.

Chinwe, in contrast, exercised regularly and always made sure she had a balanced diet that included plenty of fresh fruit, nuts and vegetables. Her mother was the same. Chuka's dad, however, hardly did any exercise at all, except for when he tended to his garden or walked from his armchair in the parlour to the fridge. Sometimes he didn't even do that, he would just order one of his children to bring the food to him. He didn't have his son's 'sweet tooth', but he did eat a lot of fatty foods and red meat. His wife tried to steer him towards fruits, nuts and vegetables but he only wanted to eat them if they were either fried, salted or drenched in excessive amounts of palm oil. As a result, though he was small in stature, he was quite rotund as well - just like Chuka. In many ways, Chuka's family was - like mother-like daughter and like father-like son.

One ordinary day, however, would trigger a chain of events that would change Chuka's life forever…

Dad called the family together for a meeting. "Chinwe, Chuka. Come to the parlour please. Your mother and I have some important news to tell you!" he called, in the direction of their bedrooms.

"I guess Kanu, Jay-Jay Okocha and the Super-Eagles will have to wait a few more minutes before thrashing Brazil in the World Cup Final," Chuka thought to himself, as he paused the videogame and begrudgingly made his way to hear what his father had to tell him. As he trudged past a window, the usual wet season weather greeted his eyes and his ears, so much so that his footsteps on the tiled floor of the hall were drowned out by the sound of the rain tip-tapping on the window.

Chuka and Chinwe slumped onto the family sofa, as their mother began to speak: "Children, I know during the summer holidays we usually take a family vacation abroad. And this year we planned to go on a safari trip to Kenya but, unfortunately, we've had to change our plans."

"Oh my gosh! Why?" asked Chinwe, leaning forward and narrowing her eyes as if the sun had just appeared in the sky, peeked through the blinds and dazzled her.

Chuka's eyes, on the other hand, widened like a night-hunting Tarsier that had just spied a mouth-watering moth. He quickly glanced over to his father. "D-a-a-a-d?! What's mum talking about?!"

Dad tried to calm the situation by gently gesturing downwards with his hands and responding in a soft tone. "Now, now kids. It's nothing to worry about. Your mother and I just need to travel to Port Harcourt to find out why our shipping container hasn't been allowed through customs. We've had no luck over the phone, so we need to go there ourselves to sort it out."

"I'm really sorry kids but with the time and effort we put into trying to get this sorted out, we just didn't have the time to book the holiday. *And* because we'll lose lots of money if we don't get this container through customs, we can't afford to spend hundreds of thousands of Naira on trips abroad at the moment. I hope you understand," said mum.

"Nooooooo!" wailed Chuka, falling to his knees and clasping the back of his head. "Why me? Why me?" he thought. How could he tell people that he didn't travel abroad during the school holidays? How would he ever live it down? Swift action was needed to avert this catastrophe of biblical proportions from occurring.

"Come on mum. There must be a way to sort this out and still have time for the trip. I'll help. What can I do to help? Just tell me what to do and I'll do it! Please -" pleaded the terrified teenager, still on his knees.

"I'm afraid it's not that simple," interrupted his father, walking towards his son, lifting him from the floor and ushering him back to the sofa. "This is an emergency situation and we have to take immediate action to resolve it or we could lose millions of Naira."

Finally getting her chance to speak, Chinwe asked, "This *does* sound serious. So are we coming with you or...?"

"We were just coming to that," said mum, sitting down between her children and putting her arms around them. "As you know your father and I have always spoken to you about our wishes for you to join the business when you are old enough," she explained, making sure that she gave each child equal attention by constantly glancing from one to the other. "Chinwe, because you're eighteen, *you* will be coming with us to Port Harcourt to get an understanding of the real-life ups and downs of running your own business."

"Yes!" cried Chinwe, 'fist-pumping' her delight.

Kneeling down in front of her son and taking his hands in hers, mum continued, "Chuka, because you're only thirteen, you will be staying with your grandparents in the village. Just until we get things sorted."

The news hit the teenager like a sucker-punch to the gut. This was truly adding injury to insult.

"Anyway," dad quickly interjected, sitting next to Chuka. "What would be so awful about staying with my parents for a week or so, while we get this all wrapped up?"

Chuka looked up from the speckled black and white tiled floor he had been staring at for what seemed like eons, as if therein somehow lay the answer to his current predicament. He fixed his gaze squarely at his father. "Do you know what I remember about my last visit to grandpa Kelechi and grandma Nneka? Do you?"

"Err...no," his dad responded.

"I'll tell you what I remember about that visit!" continued the agitated adolescent. "*Nothing!* I remember absolutely *nothing* about that visit!"

"I'm confused," said mum. "How can you remember *nothing*? It was only a few months ago."

"What I remember," Chuka replied, "is that there was nothing to do. Nothing to play. Nothing! No WIFI, no games consoles, no satellite channels, no tablets and no sweets or cakes allowed in the house! Nothing!"

"Okay, okay. I'll give you that. Dad is a bit strict when it comes to having technology and processed food in the house," said Chuka's father, nodding his head subtly. "But maybe this time you could spend a bit more time outside? You know? In the fresh air and sunshine."

The bemused boy stared at his father for a moment, before saying: "You really don't know me at all. Do you?"

Before he could respond to his son's cutting remarks, Chinwe patted him on the back and gestured with her eyes, that she wanted a chance to try and calm her brother down.

"You'll be alright," she said softly, putting her hand on her distraught brother's shoulder. "It'll only be for a short while and then we'll all be back home again."

"Easy for you to say," hissed Chuka, pulling his shoulder away from his sister's outstretched hand. "You're going to be staying in a five-star, air-conditioned hotel room with room-service, while all this is happening."

"That *is* true," said Chinwe, the smile spreading across her face.
Seeing that self-satisfied grin on his sister's face was the last straw, and the beaten boy stormed out of the parlour and back to his room.

A little while later, his mum walked down the hall to see him.

"Can I come in?" she asked, peering round the door to find him lying on his bed with his face buried in his pillow. He didn't reply, so after a brief moment she came in, almost tripping over a pair of shorts, a t-shirt and an empty box of his favourite chocolate biscuits in the process.

Sitting on the bed next to him, whilst stroking his head, she said "We really are sorry about all this. It just couldn't be helped, you know? We'll find a way to make it up to you darling, I promise."

Chuka raised his head slowly from his pillow. He had the look of someone who had spent their entire day trying to ice-skate uphill.

"We'll be back in no time," continued mum, licking the back of her thumb and wiping the chocolate from the corner of his mouth.

"Look," she said, glancing at the clock-radio on his bedside table. It was nine o'clock in the evening. "It's getting late darling. You'd better get some sleep. You need to get up early tomorrow because we're leaving for the village at seven."

Chuka was now sitting upright on his bed with his hands on his lap, not moving, not saying anything, just staring at his hands. "What was there to be said?"

he thought. The decision had been made and there was nothing he could do to change it.

"I love you darling," said mum, kissing his forehead and stroking his cheek.

"…Love you too," he replied, not making eye contact.

Soon after she left, Chuka began imagining just how boring the next seven days were going to be. "This is going to be just like the last time," he thought. "It'll be a monstrously monotonous Monday, a totally tedious Tuesday, a wantonly wearisome Wednesday, a thoroughly thrill-less Thursday, a fundamentally flat Friday, a stupefyingly stale Saturday, ending with a sanity stricken Sunday."

He couldn't possibly suspect how very different events would be this time around…

Chapter Two - Goodbye To Old Friends

Using his binoculars, Chuka finally saw what the cheetah was spying in the distance. It was a couple of warthog piglets playing with their family.

"Did mum remember to pack the ham sandwiches?" he thought to himself, before his attention was taken by a herd of galloping zebras.

"Lions!" yelled his father suddenly.

Chuka's mum, Chinwe and everyone in the open-top jeep immediately pointed their binoculars in the direction he was looking.

Several metres away, were two large male lions, with full, flowing manes, patrolling an area close to the zebras. The predators did not give chase. Perhaps because the heat of the blazing sun. Instead they sought the shade of a small tree and proceeded to lay down and groom each other. As the warm breeze changed direction, they halted the hygienic help and began staring intently at the safari group, having caught their scent on the wind. Because they looked so close through his binoculars, Chuka's heart took a little hop, skip and jump at the sight of these two magnificent meat-eaters gazing in his direction.

The larger of the two big cats lifted itself up with its front legs, raise its head, open its mouth and let out a massive - "Chuka! Are you up yet?!"

Monday, 6:13a.m was illuminated on his clock-radio like an unsolicited text message. He noticed the sliver of light coming from under his bedroom door, whilst the sound of his parents hustling and bustling outside his room told him that it would soon be time to go. Having to get up so early was just *one* of the many things Chuka hated about going to the village. Another was just how long it took. Almost an hour stuck in the car with only his tablet for entertainment. He would even have to hand that back to his parents when he arrived, since his grandpa did not allow such devices in his house. It was going to be a long day and an even longer week.

Just as Chuka closed his eyes again, in an effort to get a few more minutes in bed, his dad, who was already dressed, rapidly knocked on his door, opened it and said "good morning Chuks."

"Good morning dad," Chuka muttered, peaking through the sheets.

"Time to go young man. Go shower and get ready please."

When he finally out of bed, Chuka dragged his feet every step of the way from his bedroom to the bathroom, doing a brilliant impression of a sloth that had just been told by its doctor to take life at a slightly slower setting.

Chuka was the last at the kitchen table. His sister and parents were already having porridge with raisins and bananas. Breakfast for Chuka always followed the same pattern. Something sweet, followed by something sweet, finished with something sweet. And washed down with something sweet. His lunch and dinner followed the same sugary standard. He often spread so much jam on his bread that is was a running joke for Chinwe to ask him: "Are you going to have some *bread* with that *jam*?" Sometimes he dispensed with the bread altogether and just ate the jam straight out of the jar with a spoon. Other staples in his diet were fried chips with plenty of sugary ketchup or fried white bread with lots of margarine.

Today, his breakfast consisted of strawberry-flavoured milk, frosted flakes and refined white sugar. His eyes expanded exponentially, his mouth moistened markedly and his taste buds tingled tremendously as he drenched the sugary corn snack with pink-coloured cow juice and mixed the honeyed concoction together into a sticky, sickly salmon-stained slop.

Just as he started to slurp his first syrupy mouthful, Chinwe remarked: "You know it'd be much easier to just attach a sugar solution drip directly into your veins."

"You can really do that?" asked Chuka, his eyes widening in expectation.

Chinwe rolled her eyes. "I'm kidding, you twit."

Chuka squinted his eyes and poked out an even pinker than usual tongue at his sister.

After breakfast, everyone brought their suitcases out to the driveway, where dad was waiting to load them into the car. Chuka had already put his suitcase in the boot, which appeared a bit strange to his dad, because in all the time he had known him, the heaviest thing Chuka had ever carried was a grudge.

As he pushed his son's suitcase to one side, it felt a bit on the heavy side for one packed for only seven days.

"Err...Chuks. What have you got in here?" asked dad, setting the suitcase back down on the driveway.

"What do you mean?" asked Chuka, coming out of the front door. "It's just my clothes and stuff for the week."

"Yeah, I'm not too sure about that," said dad, opening the suitcase and pulling aside the clothes to reveal...a smart-phone, a tablet, a handheld games console with several games, a portable DVD player with assorted discs and a pair of over-the-ear headphones.

"Come on Chuks, you know your grandpa doesn't allow things like this in his house. You've got the basic handset I gave you to keep in touch. That'll have to do," said dad, handing the gadgets to mum, who took them back into the house.

"Foiled again," thought Chuka, as he went to sit in the back seat of the family saloon.

"I told you it was too much stuff, but would you listen...?" said Chinwe, getting in next to him.

After only triple-checking the gates to the compound, dad climbed into the car and began the long drive to the village. Looking out the window, Chuka began to think about all the things he'd miss while at his grandparents, like his friends for instance.

As they drove through the city, Chuka said a quiet goodbye to all of his closest friends, of which there were many. The first close friend he smelled through the half-open car window were puff-puff. They were being fried in a big wok at the side of the road by Ozioma, the 'patron saint of puff-puff'. She always set up her market stall at the top of his street, deep-frying those soft sweet dough balls, before sprinkling them with sugar and displaying them in a wood and glass box to hungry commuters. Driving past the stall, Chuka remembered how much he loved rolling the warm fried donuts in extra sugar and licking it off before he ate the sugary spheres, and how she always saved the crispy bits at the bottom of the wok, just for him.

Turning onto the main road, the aroma of another of his closest friends filled the air: Nigerian coconut candy. Ikenna, the 'coconut candy connoisseur' was, as always, standing by his snack cart, calling out to passers-by on the pavement and in their cars to buy his melted sugar-coated balls of grated coconut. Every Saturday, Chuka would sit on a park bench with a bag full of these candied globes. But rather than eat them, he'd suck all the sweetness out of them and spit the coconut shavings on the grass. He didn't consider it a waste because the local birds, which became synched to his weekend schedule, were always on hand to peck it all up.

Still on the main road out of Owerri, Chuka's nose caught the unmistakable whiff of his very good friend: chin-chin. Every day, on his way home from school, he would walk through the market-place to meet his crumbly companion. Neither party was ever late. The person who arranged introductions was Oluchi. Chuka would stand by her market stall and watch as she lovingly prepared the dough, cut it into little squares and deep-fried it in oil until it was crunchy and golden brown. By slightly varying the ingredients, she could even make it soft and chewy. Chuka, being Chuka, always had both versions. When the chin-chin was still hot, Oluchi would dust the extremely moreish, inch-sized pieces with sugar and nutmeg for him and he would often polish-off several bags without pausing for breath. It was ironic that Chuka's love for chin-chin, which is literally the word 'chin' doubled, was one of the main reasons that Chuka himself, had a double chin.

Now, everyone knows that you can't invite friends over without offering them a refreshing beverage. That would just be plain rude. This was how Chuka made the acquaintance of many other close friends. After eating a bag of chin-chin (especially the crunchy kind), there was nothing he liked better than - "a cold fizzy soft drink would hit the spot, right about now," he thought, noticing a supermarket in the distance.

"Dad?" he asked, as a cheeky thought popped into his head.

"Can we stop at the supermarket and buy some fruit…"

'SCREEEECH!!!' went the tyres, as dad almost lost control of the car. Mum and Chinwe turned their heads towards Chuka, like two hungry red-headed agama lizards that had just sighted some juicy flies.

"…flavoured soft drinks." Chuka finished, quietly, shocked at the result of his little prank.

The reptilian-like rendition continued, as dad, mum and Chinwe rolled their eyes like crested chameleons, when they realised that Chuka actually had no intention of eating some fruit for the first time in his life.

"Chuka!" dad bellowed, "d-o-n't do that! I almost had a heart attack."

Then mum chimed in. "What are you trying to do? Mmm? Would you rather be in hospital than spend a week with your grandparents?!"

"I'm so sorry. It was just a joke. I didn't mean for that to happen. I'm just thirsty, that's all. So can we stop and buy some drinks please?" pleaded the lamenting lad.

"No!" said mum, dad and Chinwe in unison.

Concrete, brick and glass were slowly replaced by earth, bark and leaves as they left the busy town behind them and arrived in the country-side.

"We'll be there soon, Chuka," informed mum.

But unsurprisingly, the teenager was engrossed in a game on his tablet, as he tried to squeeze every last minute of time he could get out of it, before he had to give it back. Being June and therefore the rainy season, he would have seen people on their farms weeding around their crops, greeting each other warmly as they went about their work. Chuka was more interested in the computer-generated confectionery on his tablet than the actual fruit and vegetables of the real world.

It was still early morning when they arrived at his grandparent's house, in the village of Atta. Chinedu, the young man who helped them around the house and on their farm, opened up the double gates so the car could park on the driveway. Grandpa Kelechi, a tall dark man with the body and face of a man far younger - his full head of grey hair being the only thing that gave away his age, remained standing at the entrance of the house and watched, as his extended family welcomed each other with hugs and kisses. He was not one for such displays of affection. As the former ship's captain of a commercial shipping vessel, he was a man of discipline, schedules and tradition. He always ran 'a tight ship' in his youth. Always leaving and arriving at port on time, never losing a shipment, always paying his crew on time but never allowing any tardiness or slackness from them. Now that he was older - he was seventy-three - he was much the same. But due to his age, he *walked* 'a tight ship' now.

Grandma Nneka was a sixty-eight year old, smallish, slight woman who always wore her heart on her sleeve. She was wearing a traditional red, green and gold dress and blouse, with a matching head-scarf in celebration of this unexpected visit from her son and his family. Usually she was not so fancifully dressed, as she and her husband spent much of their time tending their garden.

Back in the driveway, Chuka was busy taking his suitcase into the house, declining the help offered by a confused Chinedu, who, in all his visits to the village, had never so much as seen Chuka carry a tune, let alone a suitcase. As he reached the entrance to the bungalow, he greeted his grandpa, who greeted him in kind and patted his head. Chuka walked through the parlour, past the kitchen, towards his room at the back of his grandparent's home. He stuffed his suitcase under the bed and closed the door.

'Knock-knock'.

"Can we come in?" asked dad, opening the door.

"You're supposed to wait for an answer before you enter." said the temperamental teen.

"Sorry," said mum, closing the door. "Can we come in please?"

"Y-e-s."

"Thanks, Chuks," said dad re-entering the room. "The room looks just like I remember it."

"That's the problem," remarked Chuka with a sigh.

"Yeah. We know," said mum, giving her son a hug. "But it won't be for long. And who knows, maybe, just maybe you might have some fun this time?"

"Hi. I'm Chuka. I don't think we've met," he responded, offering his hand to his mother.

"There you go," said dad, patting his son on the back. "If nothing else, that dry sense of humour of yours will get you through the week. It'll fly by. You'll see. Now, come and say goodbye to your sister," he said, gesturing to the door.

Chuka didn't believe a word of it. As far as he was concerned, the next seven days may as well be seven months. As he walked back into the parlour, Chinwe was already saying goodbye to her grandparents.

"See you soon, bro. I'm sure you'll find a way to make things 'sweet'," she said, winking as she walked towards the front door.

"O-k-a-y?" he replied, as mum and dad said their goodbyes to grandpa Kelechi and grandma Nneka. Finally they kissed him on his forehead and waved as they made their way to the car. Chuka waved then turned to what would be his home for the week.

The bungalow was painted red and had a concrete veranda which went around all but one side of it. Within the building were four bedrooms - all of which were en suite, a large parlour and a study. Grey breeze block walls surrounded the compound which contained a concrete driveway, a large garden and a tool shed/storage barn. What it didn't have was WI-FI, satellite TV, laptops or tablets. In fact, there was no 'tech' to be found anywhere in the house except for grandpa Kelechi's old 'brick' of a mobile phone.

Chuka walked back towards the house, but wanting to avoid the half-an-hour 'words of wisdom' speech he would no doubt be receiving from his grandad, he decided to go round the left side of the house and enter his room via its door on the veranda. On his way, he found some familiar foes in his grandfather's garden: the 'objectionable' orange tree, the 'grating' guava, the 'malicious' maize, the 'unnecessary' ube, the 'galling' garden egg and the 'menacing' mango. Whenever he visited, he felt as though they were staring at him, as if they were demanding an explanation as to why he didn't like them. Shaking this feeling from his head, he made his way back to his room and locked both doors behind him. Just as he began to pull his suitcase from under his bed, there was a knock on the internal door.

"Chuka, can we come in?" asked grandma Nneka, with a smile. You could always tell if she was smiling, just by the tone of her voice. Pushing the suitcase back under his bed, he got up and let his grandparents in.

"Why was the door locked?" asked grandpa Kelechi, walking across the brown linoleum floor to the veranda entrance. "And this one too," he said, turning to face his grandson.

"Oh, leave the boy be," said grandma Nneka, putting her arm round her grandson's shoulder. "He just wants some privacy from us 'oldies'."

"Mmm-hmm," muttered grandpa Kelechi, narrowing his eyes. "Well, be that as it may, you and I need to have a talk. Please follow me to the study, young man," he instructed, exiting the room.

"Don't worry darling," said grandma Nneka, noticing Chuka's shoulders dropping on hearing his grandfather's request. "He just wants to have a little chat with you, that's all."

"So no thirty minute speech on the vices of technology, the value of hard work and the benefits of a healthy lifestyle?" asked Chuka, with a raised eyebrow.

"Well...yes. That too probably," replied grandma Nneka with a chuckle, as they walked together, her arm still round his shoulder. "Just listen to what he has to say. You just might learn something," she added, leaving him at the study door.

Chapter Three - The Agony Begins

Chuka knocked on the door.

"Come in my boy. Please sit down."

The functional décor of light-brown linoleum flooring, white painted walls and simple wooden furniture reflected grandpa Kelechi's character perfectly. It had two windows - one looking onto the driveway and the other onto the garden and that 'objectionable' orange tree. The bookshelf in one of the corners of the room had several books on history, geography, politics and economics. Fiction did not interest grandpa Kelechi. He was rumoured to have once remarked that 'fiction is nothing but falsehood, fake and a 'flim-flam'. Why would I forsake my funds for such fraudulent, phoney, forgeries?' On the wall without a window or door, hung the original university degrees of all his children. Chuka sat on a small sofa beneath the certificates and grandpa Kelechi in front of him on the only other chair in the room.

"Chuka, I understand that being here is difficult for you. I know you like your video games, your satellite TV and your junk food. And *I* know that *you* know that we do not have such things here," he stated with effortless authority.

"That being said," he continued, standing as he spoke. "I believe this experience will be good for you." He turned to look out the window facing the garden. "I have decided that, as your grandfather, I have a responsibility to teach *you* some responsibility. To that end, whilst you are here, you'll be helping out on the farm, working with Chinedu to keep the compound clean and helping your grandma prepare meals in the kitchen. You will learn to appreciate the hand-crafted food of your ancestors and not that sugary, fatty, processed food you usually eat. If you find that you cannot live without sugar, then you will chew sugar-cane or drink sugar-cane juice instead, so at least you will benefit from the nutritional benefits of the minerals and antioxidants. I understand that all this may seem a bit harsh, but I guarantee that in the future you will look back on this and be very pleased about my decision." After he had finished his speech, grandpa Kelechi continued to look out of the window, to allow the weight of his words to sink in.

His grandfather's words did indeed weigh heavily upon Chuka. So much so, that they may as well have been made of stone and mortar. The young man's body slumped towards the floor.

"My hands weren't made for farm-work. They were made for playing video games, eating biscuits, and occasionally punching Chinwe in the arm when she gets too annoying," he thought, staring at his fleshy palms.

After what seemed like an age, grandpa Kelechi turned away from the window to face his grandson. Sensing this, he looked up and offered his grandfather the sincerest smile that he could muster. The sort of look you give someone who has just spent hours in the kitchen cooking a meal just for you and when you taste it, it's just awful but you don't want to hurt their feelings. Grandpa Kelechi took the expression on his grandson's face to be one of agreement. Not that it really mattered if Chuka agreed with him or not. His house, his rules.

"Good. So that's settled then," said grandpa, looking at his watch. "As it's still early, you can start by helping Chinedu with some chores around the house. I've already spoken to him and he's expecting you. You'll find him at the front of the house sweeping the veranda."

For a split second Chuka considered protesting his grandfather's decision, but he knew that it would be futility itself to try to get him to change his mind. This was a man who, for over forty years, had not allowed a single item of processed food or drink to enter his house. When grandpa Kelechi makes a decision, it stays made.

Chuka lifted his body off the chair with a quiet groan and went to find Chinedu, who was exactly where grandpa said he would be, doing exactly what he said he would be doing. Chinedu was a slim, sporty, sixteen year old whose family weren't as wealthy as Chuka's. His parents couldn't afford to send him to university, so the money he earned working for Chuka's grandparents helped pay for him to attend the local college where he studied agricultural science.

"Hey Chinedu. How far?"

"Fine, 'brother'," replied Chinedu, looking up from his sweeping and smiling but not pausing.

"I've been told to help you with the cleaning, so..."

"Yeah, I know," responded. Chinedu. "Mr. Akunna said you'd be helping me whilst you're visiting. Why exactly is that? You didn't the last time. In fact, you spent the entire week in your room."

"Yeah, yeah…Anyway, what do you want me to do?"

"You can start by sweeping the veranda," said Chinedu, handing Chuka a traditional Nigerian broom made from dried palm tree fronds. He accepted it with a sigh and began to sweep. By the time they had finished sweeping the entire veranda, Chuka was already out of breath and perspiring heavily. Chinedu on the other hand, being used to this kind of work, was still fresh as a daisy and dry as a bone. Just then, grandma Nneka popped out of the kitchen with some drinks.

"Shhhhh. Don't tell your grandfather," she whispered.

A positively parched Chuka pushed past Chinedu, downed his drink in three thirsty gulps then breathlessly said: "Don't...tell...him...what?"

"Don't tell him I gave you orange squash."

Chinedu, who had just finished his drink, spluttered and remarked in a low voice, for fear of being overheard by grandpa Kelechi: "Oh...my...gosh. This isn't freshly squeezed orange, mango and sugar cane juice, like you always make? I thought it tasted strange. This has added sugar and preservatives in it. Mr. Akunna will hit the roof if he finds out."

"You leave him to me," said grandma Nneka, taking the empty cups. "This stays between us three. Okay?"

"Yes, ma," the boys said together, one with far more enthusiasm than the other.

"Okay, off you go and take this with you for later." She handed Chuka a 2-litre bottle of orange squash wrapped in a cloth to conceal it from her husband. "Your grandfather and I want you to help Chinedu on the farm with the weeding and harvesting."

Despite the fact that Chuka was heading off to do more, of what he considered to be, mind-numbing chores, he had a bit of a spring in his step. It seemed that after all these years of self-inflicted sucrose seclusion, grandma Nneka had come round to his way of thinking. Chinedu was right though. Grandpa Kelechi would hit the roof *if* he found out.

"Chinedu," whispered Chuka, as the other boy fetched a metal cart from the shed. "Are you going to keep what happened with grandma Nneka a secret from grandpa Kelechi?"

"Keep what a secret?" said Chinedu, as he pushed the cart towards the front gates of the Akunna compound.

"You *know* what."

Closing the compound gates behind them, Chinedu replied, "No. Don't know what you're talking about. Sorry."

The boys walked side by side down the sunlit, tree-lined road to the community farm, as Chuka continued: "I'm talking about what just happened with grandma. You know, with the orange squash."

Chinedu stopped pulling the cart, turned to Chuka, looked him square in the eyes and said: "Chuka. I.

Told. You. I. Have. No. Idea. What. You. Are.
Talking. About. Understand!?"

A smile spread across Chuka's face, as the penny
finally dropped.

"That'll do for me," Chuka thought, his eyes
lighting up.

"So, Chinedu. What're you going to do after you
finish your studies?"

A broad smile appeared on Chinedu's face as he
answered, looking firmly ahead as if he was
visualising the future. "I'm going to go into palm oil
production for myself," replied Chinedu, as they
turned off the main road and down the grassy path
that lead to the community farm. "As you know, my
father, my brothers and I, work for papa Isioma on his
palm fruit plantation. With the money from that,
combined with what I'm earning from your
grandparents, we'll soon have enough to buy a
partnership in his farm. What about you, Chuks?
What're your plans?"

"My only plans are to make it through this week
with my sanity intact," remarked Chuka, half serious
and half in jest. "To be honest, I haven't really

thought about it," he added, picking up a stick and striking it against the metre-high termite mound that indicated that they had reached their destination.

Chuka could not conceive he ever would discover, such a captivating cultivation of colour. There were oranges, bananas, coconuts, watermelon, avocados, mangos, guava, pineapples, cucumbers, cashew fruits, lemons, soursop fruit, odara, African walnuts, grapefruit, maize, tangerines, limes, African pears, tropical eggplants, rose water apples, tomatoes, peppers, bitter leaf, ugu (fluted pumpkin) leaves, African spinach, water leaf and palm fruit, to mention almost everything. They glowed like Christmas lights, as they ripened in the sun, just waiting to be picked and eaten. Chinedu absolutely loved the place. The colours, the flavours, the textures, being out in the sun and fresh air. He didn't mind, one bit, the work he had to do to be part of all this. He let his hands gently brush all the plants, the vegetables, the bark on the trees and their fruit, as if he was meeting old friends. The sun in turn, warmed his face and arms, as if it too, was welcoming back an old acquaintance.

Chuka felt something very different. He pined for the polished, processed, perfection of the supermarket - with its straight, steel shelves saturated with sugary salutations. Not for him was the lavish array of fantabulous fruit, versatile vegetables and nutritious nuts. Not for him was the serenading succour of the sun in the sky. As far as he was concerned, the nuts, vegetables and fruit were nothing more than familiar fiendish foes and the sun, a sinister scorching stranger.

Because it was the summer holidays, lots of children were on the farm helping their parents with the work. Chinedu waved to his friends, who in turn waved back at him and Chuka. Feeling too tired to respond, the chocolate-loving child stood under the shadiest tree he could find, took a swig from his grandma's bottle and leant against the trunk.

"Careful," said Chinedu. "That's an orange tree. There are bound to be weaver ants on it." Chuka jerked himself away from the tree trunk, and did a little dance as he brushed himself down.

"Anyway," Chinedu continued, looking up at the juicy sun-ripened oranges mixed in with the rays of sunshine poking through the leaves, "we're here to work."

"Oh come on," moaned Chuka, crouching on the ground. "We just got here. Can't we just chill for a minute or two?"

"Maybe *you* can," replied Chinedu, setting the cart down. "But *I* can't. I've got chores to do. Tell you what," said the older, fitter boy, looking down at the exhausted figure of his workmate. "I'll do all the hard work, gathering the ripe produce and all you have to do is push the cart back to your grandparents. How does that sound?"

Chuka, who in his fatigued state, would have agreed to just about anything, if it meant he could relax for a while longer, stuck up a thumb in agreement. Several minutes later, he just about garnered enough strength to raise his frame from the ground and take a second swig from the bottle. As he salivated, savoured and sucked down the sweet solution, he looked to see how Chinedu was getting on. He could hardly believe what he was seeing. Chinedu appeared to be gliding from plant to plant, like a honey bee floating from flower to flower carefully collecting nectar to take back to its hive. Chinedu, seeing that Chuka was now standing, waved at him as he went about his work. Chuka noticed an older boy, who he recognised as Chinedu's elder brother, running towards his younger sibling. He said something to him and rushed off in the same direction from whence he came. Chinedu hurried over to Chuka, leaving the cart where it stood.

"Sorry, but I'm urgently needed at papa Isioma's farm. I have to cover for a sick worker, so you'll have to take the produce home without me. You know the way, right?"

"Y-e-s, but why should I have to carry all that stuff home by myself?" asked Chuka.

"You agreed to. Remember? Besides, I didn't have enough time to get everything so it's only half-full. Okay?" And with that, Chinedu raced after his brother and was soon out of sight.

The other people on the community farm were starting to leave too, as it was getting close to twelve o'clock and the intense heat of the midday sun. Squash bottle in hand, Chuka made his way towards the cart. He pushed the cart for about a metre before stopping.

"Why should I have to push this home all by myself? I'm not a farmer," he thought. Then a smile spread across his face, as an idea came to him. Earlier, he had noticed a big hole next to the orange tree he was shading under. Chuka unloaded more than half of its contents into it. He then used his feet to push the soil back over the produce, looking around all the time to make sure that no one saw him. When he was satisfied that his actions had remained unseen, he tried pushing the cart again.

"That's better," he thought, as he started to make his way back home.

Before long, Chuka began to feel a pang of guilt about what he'd done and decided to return to the grave of greenery to undo the deceitful deed. But then he felt a far more formidable and familiar pang. The pang of hunger. Within moments, thoughts of telling the truth had been tossed in the trash and before he knew it, he was already home. Opening the gates to his grandparents' compound, Chuka noticed grandpa Kelechi snoozing in the shade on the veranda. He tried to sneak past him, so as to avoid any uncomfortable questions, but the sound of the rusty cart wheels woke him up.

"Who's there?" he murmured, slowly opening his eyes. "Chuka my boy. There you are," he said, sitting up in his rocking-chair. "I received a call from your mum. They got to Port Harcourt with no problems and are currently trying to resolve the situation. They'll call you in the evening. Okay?"

Chuka kept walking. "Okay."

"How did you get on at the farm?" enquired grandpa.

"Fine, fine," said Chuka, still not stopping.

Now standing and stretching, grandpa Kelechi continued: "I heard about Chinedu having to go help on the plantation. Good for you, bringing back the farm produce all on your own."

"Thank you sir," replied Chuka.

"Hold on, hold on," said grandpa Kelechi, walking over. "Let me see what bounty mine and Chinedu's hard work has reaped."

"Is that it? Where's the rest of it?"

Eyes fixed firmly on the half-empty cart, Chuka responded: "Yeah...well you see, because Chinedu had to leave, we didn't manage to pick as much as we wanted to. Sorry."

There was a pause, during which grandpa Kelechi looked at Chuka, then the cart, then Chuka again, then the cart, then back at Chuka.

"Alright then. Put it in the shed, wash your hands and come and have lunch".

"Thanks grandpa but I'm not really hungry."

"Not hungry? It's after midday. You haven't eaten for hours. Put the cart away, wash up and come and eat. Your grandma has prepared some delicious pounded yam and egusi soup for us."

"Yes sir," droned Chuka. Once again he would have to pass the gruesome garden and all those juicy judgemental jurors. Not so long ago, he had buried their fellow fruits, vegetables and nuts for no good reason. The evidence, though now covered in mud, was still clear. Now all their goodness would be lost to the ground, instead of making a body strong and sound. As he walked past the garden, a slight wind blew through the leaves which seemed to rhyme: ♫

'All that food, all that taste, dear oh dear, oh what a waste. All that food, all that waste, and all because of Chuka's haste' ♫. Chuka hurried along, ignoring the accusatory acoustics. He dumped the cart in the shed, hurriedly washed his hands under the outdoor tap and made his way to his room, locking the doors. When he was satisfied that he was all alone, he reached under his bed and pulled out his suitcase. Inside it was the bag of sweets, cakes, biscuits and fizzy drinks he had hidden in the spare tyre well of the family car. He opened it slowly and deliberately, like an explorer who had just find a long lost treasure chest. As its precious contents were revealed his eyes expanded until they felt as though they were going to pop out of their sockets. Chuka noticed that the packet of his favourite biscuits was already open and a couple were missing. "I don't remember eating those," he said to himself, as he peeled the wrapper off and took his first bite.

Just then, the inner door flew open.

"Come on Chuka, the food…"

Chuka froze mid-crunch, as grandpa Kelechi looked down on him with his arms crossed, and the expression on his face even crosser.

Chapter Four - Grandpa Really 'Takes The Biscuit'

"Chuka!" grandpa Kelechi bellowed. "What's that?!"

"What's what?" squeaked the scared scallywag.

"What's *that*?!" said grandpa Kelechi, pointing at the bag of treats. Chuka sighed, put the half-eaten biscuit back in its packet and handed it, and the shopping bag to his grand-father. Grandma Nneka had heard the raised voices and come to investigate.

"Husband? What's the matter?" she queried.

Grandpa Kelechi showed her the shopping bag.

"Ah...well. I'll leave you boys to it. When you're done, come and have lunch. It's almost ready." And with that, she left them to their own devices.

Grandpa turned to Chuka, who was now standing, head hanging, with his hands behind his back. "My boy, I'm really disappointed in you. You have deceived your grandma and me...*and* your parents. Do you have anything to say for yourself?"

"Sorry grandpa," said Chuka, still looking at the floor.

"Do you have anything else hidden away?"

"No grandpa," said Chuka, now looking up at him.

"Are you sure?"

"Yes, grandpa."

"Okay. I believe you. We'll say nothing more about this for now. Come, let's have lunch."

"I'm sure I locked that door. Didn't I?" thought Chuka, looking behind him at it, as he followed his grandpa into the kitchen.

Grandma Nneka watched them as they entered the room and then turned back to the gas stove to tend to the pot of simmering egusi soup. The pounded yam had already been prepared, moulded into slightly flattened tennis ball shapes and placed in a large ceramic bowl with a glass cover. Grandpa Kelechi closed his eyes as the appetising aromas of the onions, chillies, melon seeds, palm oil and ground crayfish teased his taste buds.

"I'll be back in a minute," he said, popping off to the toilet.

When he returned, to his surprise, Chuka was already furiously feasting on the food in front of his face.

"Chuka," said grandpa Kelechi. "Since when do you like pounded yam and egusi soup so much?"

"Since I added my 'special tomato sauce'," replied, the now sitting grandma Nneka, smiling at Chuka, who gave her a sauce covered smile in return.

"Well I'm very pleased to hear it and indeed to see it. You'll have to pass the recipe on to his mother when she returns next week," said grandpa Kelechi, before tucking into the delectable dish before him.

"Mama," smiled grandpa Kelechi, after he'd finished his meal. "That...was...absolutely wonderful. You really are the best cook in the village."

"I wholeheartedly agree," said Chuka, licking his plate.

"You're very welcome boys," said grandma Nneka, as she began clearing up the dishes.

"No, no. Leave that," said grandpa Kelechi, gently resting his hand on hers. "Chuka will clear the table and wash the dishes, won't you my boy?"

"Yes sir," said Chuka, standing up with half a smile on his face. The sweetness of grandma's 'special tomato sauce' and the promise of more to come, gave him *some* hope that his visit wouldn't be so bad after all.

"Such gentleman. I'm off to put my feet up," smiled grandma Nneka, laying her hands on their shoulders, before heading out to the veranda.

"But before the dishes, we have the small matter of *this* to sort out, don't we?" said grandpa Kelechi, pointing to the bag of sugary treats. Chuka glanced at the bag and nodded.

"I'm not willing to disrupt the digestion of this delicious meal by discussing your deceit, so you are confined to your room until dinner-time and I will make my decision then. Okay? But first, please clear the table and wash the dishes. I'm off to join your grandma on the veranda." And with that grandpa Kelechi, bag in hand, departed the room.

When Chuka finished his chores he retreated to his room. It was now early afternoon but the weather was still humid and the warm sun was still shining through the glass louvre window. The soft mattress cradled his tense shoulders as he thought about all the fun he could be having, if only he was at home. The hours dragged on until, quite unexpectantly, grandma Nneka popped in with a plate of biscuits.

"Come on. Eat them quickly," she said, handing him the plate.

The boy didn't need to be asked twice. He scoffed the treats down in ten seconds flat, fearing a repeat of today's earlier biscuit blunder. Grandma Nneka winked at him and departed, as swiftly and silently as she had appeared.

It was dark by the time grandpa Kelechi called Chuka back to the kitchen to inform him of his decision.

"Chuka you know our rules. No processed food or drink in the house," said grandpa Kelechi, his arms out by his side with the palms facing upwards, as if he was giving thanks. "So I'm afraid I'm going to have to dispose of these items."

"No! Please!" beseeched the boy, his hands pressed firmly together in supplication. He walked towards his grandpa, hands still pressed together. "I'll do anything. I'll do the dishes, sweep the veranda, clean the house, weed the garden. I'll even dig up the fruit and veg I buried at the...." his mouth remained open, but no more sound came from it.

"What did you say?" asked grandpa Kelechi, leaning his head towards Chuka, hoping that he'd misheard him. Chuka, realising what he had said, remained silent and motionless, except for furiously picking at his fingernail.

"What were you thinking?! What a waste!" cried grandpa Kelechi. "Actually, that food will not go to waste because tomorrow, at first light, you will dig up that food, bring it home and help your grandma turn it into a delicious meal which we will all enjoy."

"Yes grandpa. I'm sorry grandpa. I know it was wrong."

Now speaking in a calmer tone, his grandpa responded: "I'm glad you understand that. Fine. We'll say no more about it and you will make amends tomorrow. Alright?"

"Yes grandpa," replied the now slightly happier young man. He knew his grandfather was not one to bear grudges.

Grandma Nneka came into the kitchen. "All settled now boys?"

"All sorted," replied her husband.

With that, they all chuckled and sat down for a dinner of roasted plantain, roasted yam, scrambled eggs and grandma Nneka's 'special tomato sauce'.

After dinner Chuka spoke to his parents, keeping the trials and tribulations of the day to himself for now. They had enough to contend with at the moment, he thought. He even managed a few kind words to his sister - his first of the year.

Once Chuka was in bed he quickly fell asleep, exhausted by the day's events. He was only awakened at midnight by the sound of thunder and heavy rain as the heavens, having threatened to do so all day, finally shed their heavy load.

Chapter Five - The Fruits (And Vegetables) Of No Labour

The piece of cake was so soft that Chuka barely had to chew it. Instead, he used the roof of his mouth and his tongue to mould the triple-chocolate treat into balls that he sucked, like boiled sweets, till they were gone. As he ate, he half-closed his eyes as if in some kind of trance as the chocolate flavours caressed his palate – first dark, then milk and finally white. All his troubles, like the chocolate, just seemed to be melting away. The moment would be absolutely perfect if it wasn't for that really annoying noise in the background...

"Come on boy! Time to go!"

Chuka peeled his face off his saliva-soaked pillow and looked up to see grandpa Kelechi standing in the bedroom doorway. Attempting to wipe the saliva from his face, his finger got caught on a 'drool crust' as thick and hard as the short-crust pastry from his mother's apple pie. He used his hand to move the crust away from his lips - usually it was the other way round.

"Time to get up Chuka!" boomed grandpa Kelechi. "Those fruits and vegetables won't dig themselves out of the ground."

Chuka arrived in the kitchen just as grandma Nneka was serving up hot bowls of akamu. He usually didn't like the somewhat sour taste of pap but, sure as 'eggs is eggs', grandma Nneka was adding 'something special' to his bowl.

"Good morning Chuka. How're you feeling?"

"A little tired," he replied, struggling to keep his eyes open.

The akamu went down a treat thanks to grandma Nneka's added ingredients and soon Chuka and his grandfather were on their way to the community farm. Opening the front gate, grandpa Kelechi greeted the dustbin men as they went about their duties, whilst Chuka silently bemoaned the loss of his bag of treats. Walking along the main village road, cart in tow, Chuka noticed how clean and shiny all the leaves were after last night's downpour. The damp soil and vegetation lent a fresh and fragrant air to the surroundings, which helped to lift his spirits despite the reason for them being out in the first place.

Once again, they passed by the termite mound which was now a darker shade of brown. Surrounding it was a carpet of glassy wings, shed after the previous night's frivolities.

Even though it was early in the morning, the farm was very busy. People had taken advantage of the wet conditions do some weeding. The sodden soil making it a much lighter task than usual.

When they arrived at the orange tree they saw that the hole was empty.

"It was definitely there grandad. I promise," remarked Chuka, pointing at the ground.

Grandpa Kelechi looked around his plot and went to talk to other farmers, to ask if they had seen anything but he could find nothing, and no one knew anything. Not being one who gives up easily, he decided to go to the village hall to try and find some answers. As he was about to leave, Chinedu arrived. He and Chuka set about weeding the plot and harvesting the remaining fruit and vegetables. Even though it was hard going, Chuka felt less tired than last time and carried out the work without too much complaining. Unfortunately for him, just like yesterday, Chinedu had to go and help his family on the palm fruit plantation. As he pushed the cart home, Chuka grumbled a little under his breath about how difficult it was but, truth be told, he found it a little bit easier than before.

Back at the house, he noticed what looked like a scarecrow in the garden. It was unlike any scarecrow that he had ever seen. Not that he had seen many scarecrows before, living in the city, save ones in books and on TV. Nevertheless, he could see that someone had put a lot of effort into creating this unique effigy. Standing around eight feet tall, its feet were king-sized cassavas, its lower legs were huge 'hairy' yams and its thighs were gigantic fluted pumpkins. The torso was a combination of two weighty watermelons, with an overgrown pineapple for a head. The upper arms were made of massive paw-paws, the forearms were enormous yellow plantains and its hands were a pair of mammoth mangos. Not being able to make out the fingers of the scarecrow, as it had its back to him, Chuka moved in to take a closer look.

"Wow. This is really incredible. I wonder who-"

"Shhh. I'm trying to listen to this overly oratory and opinionated orange tree over here."

Chuka froze and then looked around to see where the words were coming from.

"Pssst. Up here," said the voice again.

Chuka looked up slowly to see that the pineapple head had turned round one hundred and eighty degrees, and was smiling down at him.

"Ahhhhhhhhhh!!" Chuka screamed, as he ran towards the house.

He found grandma Nneka in the parlour reading a book.

"Grandma, grandma. The scarecrow is alive!" he shouted, pointing in the direction of the garden.

"Scarecrow? What scarecrow?" she replied, closing the book and furrowing her brow.

"The scarecrow in the garden by the orange tree!" explained her grandson. "It even spoke to me!"

"Spoke to you?" repeated grandma Nneka, with a bit of a grin. "You probably just heard our neighbours talking on the other side of the wall."

"No. No, it wasn't," persisted Chuka, taking his grandma's hand. "Come see for yourself if you don't believe me."

From the safe distance of the veranda, Chuka pointed in the direction of where he had seen the fruity figure.

Grandma Nneka, seeing nothing but trees and plants, turned to her grandson and said: "I just see the garden. It was probably just a trick of the light and, like I said, people talking on the other side of the wall. Okay, darling?"

Still holding his grandmother's hand, Chuka walked up slowly to the garden to take a closer look. There *was* nothing there.

"I...guess you're right," he conceded, looking all around him.

"Maybe it's all the manual work you've been doing lately. You're not used to it," suggested grandma Nneka, touching Chuka's forehead with the back of her hand. "Perhaps the strain of it all has got you seeing things."

Still holding his hand, grandma Nneka led him back to the house.

"Go wash up and come have something to eat. It's about lunchtime anyway," said grandma Nneka. I'm making fufu and okro (okra) soup.

"With 'special sauce'?" asked Chuka, with a grin.

"Yes. *With* 'special sauce'," confirmed grandma Nneka, as they made their way back to the house.

"I've just been working too hard. Simple really, when you think about it," Chuka thought, washing his hands and face in his sink. "Some of grandma's cooking and I'll be as good as new."

"That was a bit rude. Screaming and running off like that. You didn't even introduce yourself," a voice from behind, suddenly complained.

"Not again!" yelled Chuka, not even looking behind him as he ran to the kitchen. "It's in my room! It's in my room!"

Once again, grandma Nneka went with Chuka to see the 'scarecrow', and once again, there was no one there. This time she decided that it would be best if he stayed with her, so they both went to the kitchen to enjoy the fufu and okro soup.

As they were about to start eating, grandpa Kelechi returned from the village hall. He'd had no luck. No one knew anything about the buried fruit and vegetables.

"It's all a bit of a mystery," he confessed, washing his hands.

When grandpa Kelechi was sitting, Chuka told him, with the passion of a Malian Griot, all about the strange goings-on. He narrated with such energy that every noun noted, struck with the rhythm of an Udu pottery drum. Every verb vocalised, tooted smoothly like an Oja wooden flute. Every adjective announced, thumped aggressively, like the expert pounding of an Igba cylinder drum. Every adverb articulated, chimed and signalled with the tempo of an Ogene gong. And every pronoun professed, beat in perfect time as if played out on an Ekwe slit drum. While listening to Chuka's musical message, Grandpa Kelechi's eyes flickered in all directions, like the gyrations of a traditional Igbo Mmanwu masquerade dancer.

Grandpa Kelechi stared at the kitchen table, without really seeing it, whilst he pondered the peculiar predicament. After a short while he said: "Let us eat first. It is not good to make decisions on an empty stomach."

After the meal, everyone took their seats on the veranda. Even in the shade it was still warm, so Chuka's grandparents took their raffia fans with them to try to stave off the heat of the day. The high sun cast short shadows on the ground as grandpa Kelechi prepared to deliver his verdict. Before he spoke however, he reached under his chair and took out a clear, glass bottle half-filled with a cloudy white liquid. He poured some of it on the ground before drinking a little himself. Grandma Nneka explained that the reason grandpa Kelechi had poured some of the palm wine on the ground was as an offering of respect to their ancestors.

Finally, grandpa Kelechi spoke. "I believe, from what you have told me, that what you saw is an 'Arusi.' "

"I agree," added grandma Nneka, nodding with her eyes closed.

"What's an Arusi?" inquired Chuka, leaning forward in his chair.

Continuing to fan himself, grandpa Kelechi illustrated: "In Igbo culture, the Arusi are the goddesses and gods of the elements of land, water, fire and wind. They control these elements of nature and help to keep everything in balance."

"Kind of like Mother Nature," explained grandma Nneka.

"Are you serious? You can't be serious," remarked Chuka.

"I'm very serious," said grandpa Kelechi. "There's no other explanation."

Chuka leant back in his chair and looked up at the sky as he tried, in vain, to recall a time when his grandfather had cracked a joke or told a tall tale.

"So what do they want from me?" he finally asked.

"We don't know," replied grandma, reaching over to Chuka and placing a reassuring hand on his arm. "But we do know that they act as guides and advisors, so they're here to help."

"They must have come to give you some important information my boy," clarified grandpa Kelechi, leaning back in his chair and sipping his wine.

"Okay. So if or *when* it appears to me again, I just listen to what it has to say?"

"That would be the best course of action," agreed grandpa Kelechi.

Chuka looked around the compound, half expecting the 'fruity fiend' to appear at that very moment. When it didn't, he decided to stay with his grandparents on the veranda, as they played a game of 'Ayo' and talked about the ancient history of the Igbo people.

Even though his dinner of moi-moi and dried fish had been smothered in grandma Nneka's 'special tomato sauce', Chuka did not consume the food with his usual relish. Instead he picked at it and from time to time ate tiny morsels - endlessly chewing the miniscule mouthfuls until they had the consistency of baby food. Seeing what was happening, grandma Nneka offered him some encouraging words: "Chuka, I understand that you don't want to be on your own but from what you've told me, the Arusi only comes when you are alone. Delaying things won't help, you know."

"Yeah, I know," Chuka acknowledged, still picking at his food.

After he finally finished his dinner, Chuka spoke to his parents. Grandpa Kelechi thought it best that he not divulge the day's extraordinary events to them, as they wouldn't believe it anyway and it would just worry them needlessly. So he kept it to himself.

Chapter Six - A Sweet And Savoury Fantasy

Chuka slowly peered round the bedroom door. No one was there. He took one last glance towards the kitchen, where his grandparents were standing and smiling at him, before weakly smiling back at them and closing the door behind him. Despite the 'scarecrow's' two earlier appearances, there was no sign of it this time. Weary from the day's adventures, Chuka sank heavily onto his bed. As soon as his head hit the pillow, it appeared in front of the bedroom door. He was just about to call out to his grandparents, but remembering his grandfather's words, he managed to curtail this desire. Moonlight shone faintly through the gaps in the blinds, as Chuka tried to make out the shape in the gloom. It looked different somehow. It was the same height and build, but something about its appearance was strange. Well, stranger. Chuka sat up in his bed, took a deep breath, mustered all his courage and turned on his bedside lamp. It certainly *was* different, and in a good way. Scratch that. It was different in a *great* way!

"That's a new look for you," smiled the surprised son.

"New look?" queried the creature. "Oh. I get it. You think I'm Frankie. Don't you?"

"Err, yes, err, no, I...who's Frankie now?"

"Frankie or 'Fruity Frankie', as I like to call her sometimes, is the Arusi you originally met out in the garden. My name is Zabrina. I'm a totally different Arusi. And in case you were wondering. Yes. I'm a 'her' too," she explained.

"O...K...So grandad was right. Should I expect any more? Or is it just the two of you?"

"It's just the two of us," clarified Zabrina. "I'm sure Frankie will be arriving by and by. Anyway, while we're waiting, what do you think about *my* look? This is just one of many I've tried. I'm pretty sure you weren't too impressed by Frankie's," she said, giving Chuka a twirl.

Chuka didn't really hear what she said. He was too busy clocking the copious collection of candy to concentrate on the question. Her head was a two-litre bottle of orangeade with red strawberry laces growing from the top. The upper half of her torso was a huge donut ring covered with multi-coloured sprinkles. Completely filling the centre was an extra-large pepperoni pizza. Her arms were jumbo-sized, tri-coloured fizzy drink cans, with the words 'Z-COLA' in bold letters across them. Her palms were sticky cinnamon rolls with dark and milk chocolate fingers for, well, fingers. The lower half of her torso was also a huge donut ring, but this one was covered in a red and white sugar glaze. Completely filling the centre was a colossal chocolate-chip cookie. Finally, her legs were extra-long candy striped canes that curled into balled feet at the end.

"So what do you think?" she asked again, completing her twirl.

Chuka's eyes were just as glazed over as the donut rings and his tongue was too busy dripping substantial sums of saliva on the bedroom floor, to be of any use.

"Hello?" she persisted, snapping her chocolate fingers in his direction.

"This must be what angels look like," Chuka thought, out-loud.

"What?"

"Nothing, nothing," said the child, shaking his head. "Umm. Am I dead? Is this heaven?"

"My dear boy," she remarked, taking a hesitant step towards the seated sibling. "No and no. You are very much alive. Okay?"

"Of course I am. Sorry. Silly question," said Chuka, touching his face and the bed, just to be sure.

"That's alright. Anyway, you hungry?" Zabrina asked, breaking off a piece of the colossal cookie and offering it to the boy.

"That is soooooooo disgusting.....*ly delicious*!" laughed Chuka, as he got off his bed to accept the creepily cannibalistic confectionery.

Stepping down from his bed, his bare foot slipped on the spill of spittle and he spiralled head first towards the floor. His hand was thankfully caught, just before he slammed face first into the floor. Opening his eyes, he saw that the hand that had saved him was not a cinnamon roll with assorted chocolate finger fingers, but a large ripe, juicy mango hand with banana, carrot, ube, okra and palm fruit fingers. He looked up to see, the now strangely familiar sight of an overgrown pineapple smiling down at him.

"Frankie? Umm...thank you," remarked Chuka, side-stepping his spittle.

"That's ok. Happy to help," she replied, standing at the bottom of the bed.

"Now that we're all here, I believe some explanations are in order. Don't you Zabrina?" suggested Frankie.

"Before we get to that, where are we on the cookie? Still want some?" asked Zabrina, offering it again to the addicted adolescent.

Chuka hesitated for a moment, his face contorted in thought, as he was caught between really wanting more information and really wanting the sugary snack.

"Come on Z. We don't have all day," remarked Frankie, delivering Chuka from his dextrose dilemma.

"Fine, fine," huffed Zabrina, moulding the cookie pieces back into her body.

"Now *that* is disgusting...and disappointing," said Chuka, watching what he wanted being whisked away.

"I guess that's just the way the cookie 'un-crumbles'," joked Frankie.

Chuka and Zabrina exchanged frowns.

"Anyway, explanations. Okay. This body was created from contents of the bag of sugary treats your grandfather threw away, which ended up on the dump with the rest of the rubbish. Oh, and a little bit of Arusi magic too, naturally," explained Zabrina.

"Naturally," responded Chuka. "Come to think of it, I thought those cinnamon rolls looked familiar. Not to mention the candy canes, the donuts and the cookie. I don't remember them being *quite* so big though. Also, I'm pretty sure I didn't come to my grandparent's house with an extra-large pepperoni pizza. That would be way too conspicuous."

"Here's the thing. I decided to 'SUPER-SIZE' myself. You know how it is. Don't you Chuka?" smiled Zabrina, winking at him. "And the pizza? Just a little something I added myself. I was feeling a little empty and wanted a little savoury sumthin' sumthin' to fill a hole. I mean before I got that pizza, I was so skinny you could see right through me," she laughed.

"Thanks Zabrina," said Chuka. "You actually answered a quite a few questions for me. You've left me with, like, a thousand more, but you know, small steps…Okay, Frankie. What's your story? Wait…is that a dress?"

"Oh yeah," Frankie replied, checking herself out. "I was advised by that orange tree, that my look could be construed as, well, being naked. So…do you like it?" she asked, showing off the bitter leaf, ugu leaf and spinach leaf dress that covered her from her neck to her knees.

"It's…great?" shrugged Chuka, not really knowing how to respond.

"Thank you. And may I say, it's good to finally meet you without all the screaming," she smiled. "So like your grandfather told you and Zabrina mentioned, we are Arusi."

"Umm, how do *you* know what my grandpa told me?"

"We hear things. And, you know…magic," replied Frankie.

"Hang on," interrupted Zabrina. "I'm feeling a little underdressed too. And in a flash, she was

79

covered from the top of her sprinkles donut to the bottom of her striped donut, with hundreds of red and silver coloured crisp packets. "I do like a bit of bling," she remarked, admiring herself in the wardrobe mirror.

"Anyway," Frankie continued. "This body came into existence on the night of the thunder storm, when I used Arusi magic to animate the pile of fruit and vegetables you buried in the community farm."

"Obviously. Of course. I get it. You know this kind of stuff happens to me every week," remarked Chuka.

"It does? Really?" asked Zabrina.

"No!" cried Chuka. "It doesn't. Giant 'Sucrose Zombies' generally do not appear in my bedroom in the middle of the night and offer me massive pieces of chocolate-chip cookies, that just happen to be part of their bodies! Don't you guys know sarcasm when you hear it?!"

"No, not really," replied Frankie. "That's one of those tricky human quirks we find a little hard to master. Perhaps you can teach us?"

"Teach *you*?" laughed the lad. "I thought you were here to teach *me* something?"

"Oh...yeah. Sure. We'll do that too," assured Frankie.

"Do you mind if we sat down first?" asked Zabrina.

Two seats appeared. Zabrina's was a humongous pink and white striped marshmallow, which sounded as if someone had dropped a massive bag of marbles on the floor when she sat on it.

"Jellybeans?" asked Chuka.

"Gob-stoppers," grinned Zabrina.

Frankie's chair was a massive mango - on its side, with enormous ube arm-rests and another massive mango as the back. As Frankie sat down, the ripe mango seat 'gave' like a soft mattress when you laid on it.

"That looks really comfy, Frankie. Can I try it?" asked Chuka.

"Hey Z. The *man* over there would like to have a *go* on my chair," laughed Frankie.

"Hilarious," groaned Chuka, staring at Frankie with his arms akimbo.

"Sarcasm?" asked Zabrina.

"Sarcasm," nodded Chuka.

"I knew it!" shouted Frankie. "I told you we were quick learners. Okay. Here's your chair."

An exact but smaller copy of Frankie's mango chair appeared next to the bed. Chuka reclined in the plush giant mango, adjusting his bottom on the soft ripe skin. "Thanks Frankie. So now that we're all comfortable, will somebody please tell me why you guys are here?"

"Gladly," replied Frankie. "I'll go first. I'm here because we're worried that if you continue with your 'not exercising, eating loads of processed foods and not eating *any* fruits, nuts and vegetables lifestyle', you're going to get really, really ill - really, really soon."

"Ill? Ill?" chortled Chuka. "What're you talking about? I'm as fit as a fiddle. Look!"

Chuka began doing star-jumps in the middle of the bedroom.

"Woo-hoo! Look at him go!" exclaimed Zabrina, clapping her dextrose digits in time with his jumps.

"Told...you...fit...as...a...fid...dle," wheezed Chuka, sitting back down after managing to do a grand total of three star-jumps.

"Now *that* was definitely sarcasm," announced Frankie.

"What...e...ver," puffed Chuka, slouching deeper into the fruity furniture.

After catching his breath, Chuka asked: "Just now, you said '*we're* worried'. Who's 'we're'?"

"Your ancestors and me," clarified Frankie, now sitting with her arms placed on the arm-rests in a regal pose.

"Ancestors? What ancestors?" quizzed the teenager, slowly sitting up in his chair.

"Your ancestors. You know, like, the great-great grandparents of your great-great grandparents."

"Oh...really? They're watching me? Right now?" asked the young man, looking up at the ceiling.

Frankie laughed. "Well, they don't *spy* on people, if that's what you're thinking. They keep an eye on you and sometimes step in when you're headed for trouble. And you, my child, are headed for trouble. Serious trouble."

"Yeah, yeah, you already mentioned that but as you saw there's nothing to worry about. I'm in my prime."

"O...k...a...y," said Frankie, taking a deep breath, "let's look at this from a different angle. Zabrina, please tell Chuka why *you* are here and why you're so big."

"I don't want to," declined Zabrina, looking down at the floor.

"Fine. I'll tell him then," said Frankie, standing up.

"Alright, alright. I'll do it," conceded Zabrina, gesturing to Frankie to sit down.

"I'm a physical manifestation of your cravings for sweets, cakes, biscuits and junk food in general, and my size simply reflects the size of your appetite for these things. And I'm here because, well…you 'summoned' me."

"I summoned you?" repeated Chuka, with raised eyebrows. "Pretty sure I'd remember that."

"When Frankie was sent by your ancestors to help change your lifestyle, *you* reached out to me with your sub-conscious as a kind of self-defence mechanism, to try to keep things the way they are," explained Zabrina.

"Wow!" exclaimed Chuka. "That is a *lot* to take in. I'm going to need a little time to digest all of this."

"How about a swig of orangeade?" recommended Zabrina, removing her head from her body and offering it to Chuka. "I hear it can aid digestion."

"That's just a myth," countered Frankie, getting up from her chair. "Here, try this instead," presenting him with a piece of paw-paw from her arm.

"Guys, guys. I don't actually need to *physically* digest anything!" cried Chuka, standing up and rubbing his eyes with his palms. "I just need some time to think about things. Okay? Can you guys just go please?!"

And with that, Frankie, Zabrina and all three chairs vanished from the room, leaving Chuka to his deliberations.

The morning sun entered, uninvited through Chuka's window and impolitely woke him. Not that he slept much, as he spent most of the night thinking about Fruity Frankie's warnings about his health.

What if what Frankie said was true? What if there really was a serious illness in store for him in the not too distant future? Did he really have to trade in his sweets and treats for yucky fruits, nuts and vegetables? The thought of it made Chuka shiver, even though the temperature inside the house was twenty-five degrees Celsius. "There had to be another way," he thought. "There just had to be!" Chuka was still drowning in denial when he heard a knock on his door. For a moment he thought it may be Frankie and Zabrina, but then quickly remembered that they didn't need to use doors.

"Come in," he answered, sitting up in his bed, as his grandparents entered the room.

Seeing her grandson's blood-shot eyes and sullen expression, grandma Nneka hurried over and gave him a big hug, while grandpa Kelechi sat at the bottom of the bed with a worried look on his face.

"What happened, my son? Tell grandma all about it," she cajoled.

Chuka proceeded to tell his grandparents all about last night's conversation with the Arusi. When he was done, he asked them if *they* agreed with the Arusi, that he was headed for a dietary disaster. There was a slight pause in the conversation as Chuka's grandparents looked at each other.

"Yes," replied grandpa Kelechi, directly.

Grandma Nneka, being of softer character, replied: "No darling. No. Perhaps you could stand to eat one or two less sweets, but...no," she assured him, whilst cradling his head under her chin.

"Ah beg!" interjected grandpa Kelechi. "Can you please stop deluding the boy?! It's clear to all that he needs to stop eating all these processed foods, start exercising and eat more healthily. Listen Chuka, the Arusi wouldn't be here unless they believed you really needed their help. And this is just the first step in their education. There's more to come, of that I am certain," he concluded.

"Like what?" questioned the concerned kid.

"Like this," a hidden voice said.

Suddenly the bedroom, his grandparents, the house, everything was gone and Chuka was in what appeared to be a doctor's waiting room. The large black and white square design on the floor stretched off endlessly into the distance, which made it look like a giant chess board. Fastened to the floor were rows of metal chairs with hundreds of tiny perforations in their seats. The white painted walls were covered with healthy living posters, giving advice like: 'Want A Strong Heart? Exercise! There's A Start!'

Chuka heard a sound and turned to see Frankie sitting in the reception area.

"Hi there," she said merrily, giving him a little wave.

"Frankie! What have you done? Where am I?" demanded Chuka, walking up to her.

"You're in our world," another voice stated.

Chuka spun round to see Zabrina sitting on one of the metal chairs, smiling at him and tapping her chocolate fingers together like a pantomime villain.

"Well, you can just take me right back to *my* world please! I told you. I need some time to think about what you guys said."

"I'm afraid time is running out for you my friend. You see that poster over there?" asked Frankie, getting up and pointing to the wall.

"Which one? The one with your picture on it that reads: 'Get Your Five-A-Day - The Fruity Frankie Way'? Or the one with Zabrina advertising 'Z Orangeade' and...using a bendy straw to drink orangeade from her *own* head? ...How is that even possible?" asked Chuka.

"It's a lot harder than it looks, I can tell you," remarked Zabrina. "I almost drowned the first time I tried it."

"How did that get up there?" asked Frankie, tearing down the Zabrina poster. "No, the one next to it that reads: 'Diabetes. Are You At Risk?' "

Chuka slowly walked up to the poster. As he got closer the words morphed to read: 'Diabetes. *You* Are At Risk!' and an image of his face appeared below the text.

"What's this supposed to mean?" quizzed Chuka, frowning at Frankie.

"It means precisely what it reads," responded Frankie, now standing next to the teenager. "Being overweight and inactive are contributing factors to developing type 2 diabetes, which can lead to things like wounds not healing properly, getting sick more often and, if left unchecked, even blindness. In addition to that, I know that if you don't change your lifestyle, you will never reach your full potential in life."

"To be fair, he's not *that* overweight and inactive," said Zabrina. "After all, he did manage to do three star-jumps that time."

"Thanks Zabrina...I think," muttered Chuka, as he turned away from the poster. "Look, I'm sure your heart is in the right place...I'm sorry...Is it in the *right place*? Do you actually have a heart in there? I can't really tell."

"It's complicated," responded Frankie.

"Anyway, I bet there are loads of people throughout history that never ate fruits, nuts and vegetables who were completely healthy *and* reached their full potential in life."

"I'll take that bet!" responded Frankie, swiftly.

"Bet? What bet?" asked the confused kid.

"I bet that I can prove to you that an unhealthy lifestyle can lead to serious health issues *and* stop people reaching their full potential," Frankie clarified. "If I win, will you promise to change your lifestyle?"

"*We'll* take that bet!" yelled Zabrina, jumping up from her chair and putting her arm around Chuka.

"Hold on, hold on," protested Chuka, pulling away from Zabrina. "And if you can't prove it? Hmm? What's in it for me?"

"If I can't prove it, then I'll leave and never bother you again," answered Frankie.

"Like I said, we'll take that bet!" implored Zabrina, stretching her arm up in the air, like a student desperately trying to get their teachers attention.

"How come you're so confident?" asked Chuka.

"Yeah. Why *are* you so confident?" asked Frankie.

"Come on," said Zabrina. "Whoever heard of eating cakes and sweets stopping someone from reaching their life's full potential? It's ridiculous. This is going to be an absolute 'cake-walk'. Trust me. And when we win, I will personally make you a pair of shoes out of cake, so you can walk on a street covered in cake, while eating the shoe boxes they came in, which incidentally, will also be made out of cake."

"Okay," laughed Chuka. "I *will* take that wager and I promise to change my ways if I lose, which we won't. Right Zabrina?" said Chuka glancing at Zabrina for confirmation, who, in return, nodded in verification. And with that, he shook Frankie's fruity fingers firmly to seal the deal.

"Okay, this is how it's going to work." said Frankie. "We are all going on a trip. Three trips to be exact. Each trip will be one part of the bet. If I lose on just *one* trip, then you guys win the whole thing."

"Okaaay. Three things. Where are we going? For how long? And don't you think I should tell my grandparents first? Not to mention my mum and dad?" questioned the curious child.

"That's actually four things, if you mention the thing that you mentioned not to mention," corrected Zabrina, with a grin.

"Hey, I thought you were on my side?" responded Chuka.

"My bad," apologised Zabrina, holding her hands up in simulated submission.

"Anyway," interrupted Frankie, narrowing her eyes at them. "We'll be travelling all over this great continent to carry out three experiments on the effects of eating too much processed sugar on people's ability to achieve their full potential."

"Experiments?" queried Chuka. "You mean like chemistry?"

"Just like chemistry," confirmed Frankie. "These experiments will take a while but don't worry, it'll just be an instant as far as your grandparents are concerned. In fact, they won't even notice you've gone. Okay?" explained Frankie.

"Magic, huh?" remarked Chuka.

"Magic," said Zabrina.

"Oh, and there'll be a bit of time travel too," remarked Frankie, admiring her picture on one of the posters.

"Time travel?" repeated Chuka, staring intently at Frankie for further clarification.

"Time travel," re-stated Frankie, casually.

"Time travel?" re-repeated Chuka, looking at Zabrina.

"Time travel," confirmed Zabrina.

"O...K...So are we going into the past or to the future?" asked Chuka.

"To the past of course. The future hasn't happened yet," explained Frankie.

Chuka paused for a second, then responded: "Makes sense, I guess."

"Okay. We all good to go?" asked Frankie.

"I'm good," replied Zabrina.

Chuka glanced at Zabrina, then at Frankie, 'running the numbers' in his head on his chances. Finally, he replied: "Okay... Let's go."

Chapter Seven - How Tall Can You Build A Sugar Wall?

The city streets were heaving with people talking, trading and strolling in the warm sunny weather when the time-travelling trio arrived.

"So exactly where, and I guess *when*, are we?" asked Chuka almost immediately, leaning on the red dried earth wall of a house, as he tried to keep out of the way of all the people.

"We're actually still in southern Nigeria. *When* we are is a bit more interesting. It's around 800AD," explained Frankie.

"800AD?! You call this a 'bit of time travel'? And what have we come here to see?" asked Chuka, taking in the view of the people in their colourful garbs, as they hurried back and forth, going about their business.

"Don't worry, they can't see us," Zabrina assured him, knowing the question would arise sooner or later.

"Whoa! Apparently, they can't feel us either!" exclaimed Chuka, as a young lady, elegantly dressed in a black and yellow dress, walked right through him and off into the distance. "That was so weird. It felt as though a gust of wind blew right through me."

"You get used to it," said Frankie, watching the lady as she turned a corner.

As the group were taking in the scene of well-built and beautifully decorated houses, Chuka noticed a very official-looking man dressed in a long, white and gold shirt with matching trousers instructing several young men to make their way to the outskirts of the city.

"How come I can understand him? Wait, don't tell me. Magic?" asked Chuka.

"Now you're getting the hang of it. Come on, let's follow them," said Frankie hurrying after the men.

After several minutes, they reached the city boundary and saw what the men had been tasked to do. They were all taking part in the monumental undertaking of digging a massive trench around the city and then using the excavated soil to build up a giant wall to encircle it. The party of three walked for about a mile around the city frontier to capture the true scale of the works. There were hundreds of men working together with supervisors giving orders to groups of twenty or so.

After a while, the teenager, getting bored from all the walking, asked "So, where *exactly* are we?"

Standing with her paw-paw and plantain arms spread wide towards the heavens to emphasise the grandeur of her upcoming statement, Frankie announced, "My boy, we are in the Ancient Kingdom of Benin and we are here to witness the building of 'The Great Wall'."

"Never heard of it," confessed Chuka.

"What?!" howled Frankie. "You're telling me, as a thirteen year old Nigerian boy, you have *never* heard of the Kingdom of Benin? You didn't learn about it in school? Your parents never spoke about it?"

"Yes, no and no. Well maybe, but I probably wasn't listening. Should I have? Is it a big deal?"

"Yes, it is," replied Frankie. "Actually to be fair to you, most people's idea of ancient African history is the person who won the first series of 'Nigeria's Got Talent…' "

"Come on," interrupted Zabrina. "Let's not forget why we're here. We're here to win a bet! Remember? You can learn all about the Kingdom of Benin later."

"That's true," said Chuka, fixing his gaze on Frankie, with his arms akimbo. "You've told me *where* we are and *when* we are. Now can you tell me *why* we are here please?"

"Certainly," said Frankie. "The hundreds of workers you see behind you are constructing a defensive wall for their city. When the wall is completed it will extend for some sixteen thousand kilometres and cover six thousand five hundred square kilometres."

"Wow! I guess it really is a big deal!" remarked Chuka.

"Yeah, yeah. It's brilliant," commented Zabrina, hastily, "but you still haven't explained *why* we are here and *how* I can go about winning the bet."

"Follow me," said Frankie, as she led her companions to what could only be described as a giant cookout. There were rows and rows of tables stacked with meat, fish, yams, fruits, nuts and vegetables being cooked in large pots suspended over huge log fires. Several women were preparing meals for the workers to eat during their breaks. As one group of workers sat down to eat, another group, having eaten their fill and rested, went back to work. Everyone was working to a strict schedule and as a result the trench and wall were 'growing' at an extraordinary pace.

Turning to face her companions, Frankie said: "Zabrina, I want you to turn all that protein, complex carbohydrates, fresh fruit and vegetables into processed foods high in added sugar, saturated fat, artificial flavours, colours and preservatives. Oh, and change the water into cola while you're at it."

"Can do," said Zabrina with zeal, as she moved unseen between the cooks and workers magically changing their fresh food into cakes, sweets, buns, pies and biscuits and their water into cola.

"In case you're wondering Chuka, the food and drink won't look, taste, smell or feel any different to them. They'll just think that they're eating their regular rations," explained Zabrina as she carried out her conjuring.

When Zabrina had finished with her 'reverse food alchemy', Frankie finally explained *why* they were there. "We're going to see what happens when these workers switch to eating a diet high in processed sugar and fat and the resulting effect on the construction of this wall."

"Well, I can tell you both right now that the effect is going to be tremendous!" Zabrina boasted. "These guys won't know what hit 'em. They'll be working at double, no, triple speed in no time. You just wait."

"Yeah…yeah. That sounds about right," agreed Chuka, watching the workers as they unwittingly consumed the candy and cakes. "Hey. How come, looking at all this food, I'm not feeling even a bit hungry?"

"Because your body, and therefore your stomach and appetite, is still back at your grandparents' house. Only your 'consciousness' travelled with us through time. Get it?" clarified Frankie.

Chuka stared at Frankie, blinking his eyes several times before hesitantly saying: "…Yeah…Sure…Why not?"

"Well, we might as well get comfy," said Zabrina, as she materialised her massive marshmallow and sank into it again.

"Good idea," concurred Frankie, and with a gesture of her fruity fist, she summoned two mango chairs - one for her and one for Chuka.

"Thanks," said Chuka, as they all sat down to witness the upcoming events.

The workers carried on working at pace and even began digging and building faster than before. As soon as Zabrina saw this, she leapt out of her seat and began to brag loudly. "I told you! I told you! Just look at 'em go. When did you say the wall was completed, Frankie?"

"Estimates are around the 1400's but no one really knows for sure," she replied.

"They'll be done in about half the time by the looks of it," said Chuka.

"I wouldn't be so sure about that," disputed Frankie, leaning back in her seat.

"What are you talking about?" queried a confused Zabrina. "They even look happier than before. I'm telling you kid, we've got this in the bag!"

"It certainly looks that way," agreed Chuka, glancing in Frankie's direction.

"Wait for it," said Frankie, standing up and looking over at the workers.

"Wait for what?" said Zabrina. "Just admit that you've lost the bet."

"Have I?" smiled Frankie.

Zabrina and Chuka could only watch as the rhythmic melody of the worker's songs and the sound of metal cutting into the earth was gradually replaced by moans, groans and the clanking of tools as they fell to the dry ground. Back at the dining table, the men fought for first dibs on Zabrina's candied cuisine, adding a cacophony of slurping, burping, shouting and sniping to the musical mix. As the fists, feet and food flew, many a face found itself the frame for a flying fish or piece of fruit. Before long, the fantastic food fight turned into an all-out brawl, with not a single contestant even remotely interested in the building of the Great Benin Wall.

"What went wrong?" asked Chuka, as a coconut whizzed by his head, followed by two men chasing it.

"Yeah, what happened, Frankie?" asked Zabrina, watching the men fight over it, like it was a rugby ball.

"Chemistry happened," replied Frankie, pausing the pack of players with her pinkies.

"Chemistry? What you mean 'chemistry'," demanded the dumbfounded deity.

"I mean the chemical reactions going on in the workers bodies as they unwittingly took part in our little experiment," explained Frankie.

"Huh? I don't get it." replied Chuka, his face contorted in confusion.

"Allow me to clarify," said Frankie, sitting back down on her mango chair, her fingers interlocked as she prepared to impart her words of wisdom. "But before I do, I think we need to 'reset' this important moment in history." With everything in the Kingdom of Benin reverted to how it was before the magical meddlers arrived, Frankie began her explanation. "The workers, as you saw, had an initial rush of energy from all the processed sugar they ate.

However, because it was a simple sugar it was used up very quickly by their bodies and needed to be replaced. That's why the workers felt tired and moody, and why they needed to 're-fuel' after such a short period of time."

Observing that the workers were now digging and building with the same strength and speed that they had done originally, Frankie continued her report. "The reason these people are able to work at a constant pace over a long period of time, is because their energy comes from complex carbohydrates like yam and plantain. The sugar is released slowly throughout the day, so they don't need to constantly replace it. Finally, because of the protein and fibre they get from eating fruits, nuts and vegetables, they feel fuller for longer. Get it?"

"So basically you're saying, 'simple sugars' - bad, 'complex carbohydrates' - good?" enquired Chuka, raising his eyebrows.

"Well I'm not convinced," responded Zabrina, pacing back and forth. "It can't be that simple. I mean, I was winning and everything," she moaned, nibbling her chocolate fingers down to the biscuit.

"Actually, it is," replied Frankie. "If people ate 'complex carbohydrates' like yam, cassava, brown rice and sweet potatoes instead of 'simple sugars' like sweets, cakes and biscuits, then they'd have a more controlled and lasting source of energy and wouldn't get tired and moody so often. Anyway, shall we take a look at how things would've turned out, had we *not* stopped our little experiment?"

"Go on then," sighed Chuka.

"If you must," replied Zabrina.

"I know what'll cheer you guys up. I just thought of a brilliant joke," declared Frankie.

"Not really in the mood, to be honest with you, Frankie," said Zabrina, standing up and stretching her cola can arms over her now 'flat' soda pop bottle head.

"Me neither," said Chuka.

"No. It's funny. Really. Listen," replied Frankie, completely ignoring their comments. "What vegetable do you always have to wait in line for?

"I don't know. What vegetable do you always have to wait in line for?" answered Zabrina.

"A 'queue'- cumber. Get it?" chuckled Frankie.

"Okay, that is kind of funny," smiled Chuka.

"It was alright," muttered Zabrina, looking off into the distance.

"See. I told you," Frankie smiled. "Anyway, where was I? Oh, yeah."

Frankie waved her hand, and a total transformation of the terrain transpired. The city, the wall, the trench - they were all gone. The sound of chattering people had been replaced by the calls of birds and the chirrups of insects. Dense foliage stretched as far as the eye could see, with only a couple of huts breaking up the curtain of green with flecks of reddish-brown.

"Are you sure we're in the right place?" asked Chuka, looking up at the forest canopy.

"Pretty sure," confirmed Frankie, as she led them down an overgrown grass path.

The conversation was suddenly interrupted by the sound of loud yawning. The gate-crashing crew turned to see a large belly, followed a few seconds later, by the rest of the man, emerge from one of the huts. Cloth tied around his wide waist and hoe in hefty hand, he wheezily walked for few metres, stopped and yawned again. Then looking at the ground, shook his head, did an about-turn and walked home. On closer inspection, the only other hut in the vicinity was now home for the creatures of the forest, abandoned, it seemed, long ago, by its human occupant.

"Okay. Okay. I've seen enough. Can we go now?" asked Chuka, looking at a thick mass of webbing between the cracks in the hut wall that seemed to be the only thing keeping the structure standing.

"Yeah, you've made your point," moaned Zabrina, pulling her head out of the crumbling doorway.

"Alright, alright," smiled Frankie. "Let me show you how things *really* turned out."

Again, Frankie waved her hand.

"Here we are in The Kingdom of Benin, circa 1400AD."

They were back in the city streets again but this time it was at night. Thankfully, the huge street lamps, fuelled by palm oil, lit the way for our travellers and helped them to view the great kingdom in all its glory. The people were dressed in flamboyant colourful garments of yellow, green, red, black and gold and the houses had just as extravagant designs on their walls and columns.

Chuka noticed that the houses did not appear to have any doors and mentioned this to Frankie, who answered, "The city and its people are wealthy so there is no need to steal, hence no need for doors and locks. And as you can see, the wall is complete now," informed Frankie. "In case you were wondering, the part of the wall you are looking at now is about twenty metres high, so try not to strain your necks. And finally, before we move on, it's important to note that 'The Great Wall of Benin' and its surrounding kingdom were described, in the 1974 Guinness Book of Records, as the world's largest earthworks carried out prior to the mechanical era. Pretty impressive what people can do when they aren't gorging themselves on sweets, cakes and biscuits, isn't it?" concluded Frankie, with a grin.

"I have to say, that *is* pretty impressive," admitted Chuka, listening to distant drums and gongs, as they enjoyed the city nightlife.

"Where to next?" demanded Zabrina, seemingly unimpressed by everything she had seen or heard.

"Well since you asked soooo nicely, I'll tell you," responded Frankie. "Our next trip will take us to Ancient Kingdom of Kemet - the land of the Pharaohs, Pyramids and the Sphinx."

"I thought Egypt was the land of the Pharaohs, Pyramids and the Sphinx. Where's this 'Kemet'?" questioned a confounded Chuka.

"You really need to pick up a book every once in a while and open up your horizons," declared a disappointed Frankie.

"Yeah, Chuka! Really?!" announced Zabrina. "Sorry, sorry. I don't know where that came from. I'm just frustrated," she added, before Chuka could respond. "Can we just get on with the next part of the bet please?" she concluded, crossing her arms.

"Indeed we can," chuckled Frankie, amused by her fellow Arusi's attitude. And with a wave of her African pear finger, they were gone.

Chapter Eight - The Curse Of Candy On Concentration

"Wow! That is the bluest blue I have ever seen," gushed Chuka, as the travelling trio gazed at the seemingly never-ending Nile River. Broken reflections of the high, blazing sun sparkled like diamonds on its surface, as fishing boats sailed along on the shimmering water. At first glance, it could appear as if the fishermen's nets were trying to gather up the mirage of twinkling gems, rather than the glittering fish, on which they relied for their living.

"Incredible," agreed Frankie.

"This isn't too bad either," remarked Zabrina, looking in the opposite direction.

Chuka and Frankie turned to see what she was talking about.

The stone building must have stood at least ten metres tall with elegant cylindrical columns, designed to look like palm trees all around it. There were no doors or windows, just metres upon metres of silky curtains.

"Maybe it's some sort of temple," commented Chuka, watching the curtains gently wafting in the cool breeze, which carried along with it the sound of a muffled conversation coming from inside the solitary structure.

"Sounds like somebody's home," said Zabrina, attempting to peer into the property. "Shall we go in and introduce ourselves?"

"Shall we do what now?" asked the young man, scrunching up his forehead.

"Just kidding kiddo. They can't see or hear us. Just like in Benin."

The curtains gently brushed against Chuka's face as the time-travelling tourists made their way towards the source of the conversation. Inside the building, there were more cylindrical columns dotted throughout the structure, all covered in detailed colourful depictions of important dignitaries in the Kemetu Kingdom. Some images were carved into the stone columns whilst others were painted onto the walls, in vibrant greens, golds, blacks and reds, amongst other colours.

For several seconds, Chuka's mouth remained open, as he marvelled at the building's interior, but none of the words he had ensnared over the years managed to escape. Finally, a sentence broke free: "Like I said, this *must* be some kind of temple. Am I right, Frankie?"

"I believe you are," agreed Frankie. "I also believe that it was built for that guy sitting over there," she said, pointing to three men sitting round a carved, wooden rectangular table which was exquisitely decorated in gold leaf.

Neither Chuka nor Zabrina had to ask Frankie which of the three men she was referring to. He was on a raised platform and sat on a red, black, green and gold coloured throne-like chair, whilst the other two sat on lower stools in the same design and colours. The attire he was wearing also helped to set him apart from the other men. They all wore short, white linen kilts with colourfully decorated gold, green and red necklaces but his was much more elaborate in its design.

"Who *is* that?" asked Chuka.

"That melanated-marvel," said Frankie, looking in the man's direction, "is Imhotep - the world's first multi-genius or polymath. He was the father of architecture, mathematics, engineering, medicine, pharmacology and philosophy to name but a few of his attributes."

"I guess he must have been *pretty* smart," remarked Chuka.

"You *could* say that," replied Zabrina, shaking her head with a chuckle.

"Hang on a minute," thought Chuka out-loud, pointing in the direction of the three men. "Those guys are black, like me. Egyptians aren't Black people. Are they?"

On hearing this, Frankie decided to give the intellectually-lacking lad a brief lesson in African history. "Many modern Egyptians aren't black like you because Ancient Egypt, or Kemet as it was called by the original Black people, was invaded several times in history - by the Assyrians in 663 BC, by the Persians in 525BC and the Greeks in 332BC to name but a few. These invaders took over from the indigenous people and that is why you don't see many Black people in modern Egypt these days," explained Frankie. "However, at this moment, we are in Kemet, which by the way, literally means 'Land of the Blacks', around the year 2700BC, so everyone you will see, will be the original Black African people who founded the kingdom and this great civilisation way back in circa 5900BC," concluded the Arusi.

After pausing for a moment to absorb this new information, Chuka lamented, "I really *do* need to read a few more books," as he came to grips with Frankie's historical revelations.

"Don't sweat it too much," came the unlikely response from Zabrina, "learning about ancient history isn't most people's idea of fun either." Switching back into her usual demeanour, she asked: "Okay, now we've got the introductions out of the way, what's the second part of the bet? Mmm?"

"I thought you'd never ask," smiled Frankie. "We are here to question whether the conspicuous consumption of candy can curtail the creativity and concentration called for in the construction of the world's first pyramid - the Step Pyramid of Pharaoh Djoser. The oldest monument of its kind, still standing to this day. When completed it will consist of six 'steps' and be known as the tallest structure of its time at a height of over sixty metres."

"Another construction project?" queried Chuka, rolling his eyes wearily. "Pretty sure how this is going to turn out."

"Yeah," agreed Zabrina, scowling. "Exactly the same as the last time."

"Fear not my fellow time tinkerers. We're here to see if eating lots of junk food will affect Imhotep's ability to *design* the Step Pyramid, *not* to build it. He's the architect, not a builder."

With that revelation, Chuka and Zabrina breathed a sigh of relief.

"I have a really good feeling about this one," declared Zabrina, walking around the room with a new spring in her step.

"You do?" quizzed Chuka. "And what makes you think this is going to work out any different from the last time?"

"Because everyone knows that sugary food helps to fuel the brain. The sugar in my orangeade head alone will have this guy totally alert and 'buzzing' all day and all night. I guarantee it," she promised, nodding her carbonated head so much that it began to foam.

Despite the fact that Zabrina had been just as confident at the Great Wall of Benin, Chuka decided to give her the benefit of the doubt. Besides what did he have to lose? Oh yeah. Cakes, sweets, fizzy drinks...

"Okay, okay. But this time *I* get to choose what foods to give him," he demanded.

"Fine by me," agreed Zabrina. "Whatever deserts you demand will be delivered diligently," she added, with a chuckle.

"See. I can alliterate too, Frankie," smiled Zabrina.

"And you definitely didn't disappoint darling," laughed Frankie, returning the favour.

"Humph," responded Zabrina. "Alright, alright. Enough fun and games. Let's get to work. What do you want me to conjure up first?" she remarked, cracking her chocolate biscuit knuckles in readiness.

"We have to wait until they take a break for lunch first. Don't we? Besides, don't you guys want to take a closer look at what they are doing?" asked Frankie, walking over to the men.

Chuka and Zabrina followed at a snail's pace. Leaning over the table, they saw that the men were studying the architectural plans for the pyramid. It was drawn on a large piece of papyrus paper in black ink with markings, measurements and notes in various colours all over it.

"That's a real piece of history right there," commented Frankie, deciphering the detail of the document.

One of the men spoke: "But Imhotep, this has never been done before. How can you be sure that it is going to work?"

"My friend. How many times have we gone over the building specifications? Have either of you found any calculations therein that do not balance?" asked Imhotep. Both men looked at one another, then at Imhotep. They smiled and shook their heads.

"Good. Then it's settled. The work shall begin in a week's time. Come, let us take some refreshment."

"Now's our chance," said Zabrina. Chuka and Company followed Imhotep, as he led his colleagues to another part of the temple where food had been laid out for them on a banquet-sized table.

"Okay. What's it gonna be?" asked Zabrina, her magic fingers at the ready.

"Right. Okay. Brain-food? Brain-food?" muttered Chuka to himself. "I know, I know!" he cried, moving towards Zabrina and the banquet table, as the epiphany finally hit him. "Whenever I'm reading, which isn't often, I always have five or six packets of chin-chin and biscuits to keep my energy levels up *and* a two-litre bottle of cola too. You know, to keep hydrated. What do *you* think Zabrina?"

"What do *I* think? What do *I* think?" squealed Zabrina, dancing around the table flicking her fingers as she transmuted the bread, meat, fish, fruits and vegetables into biscuits, chin-chin and cola. "I'm thinking step aside Imhotep, 'cos there's a new genius in town!"

Close by, the sound of a mango slapping against pineapple could be heard.

Frankie let out an audible sigh. "Okay 'genius', while your continental cousins consume your conjured candy creations, why don't we have a look around this magnificent temple?"

"Yeah, why not?" responded Zabrina. "I'm just about finished here."

So the three historical hitchhikers wandered off to see the rest of the temple, leaving Imhotep and his associates to enjoy their enchanted edibles.

"Just walking through this temple makes me think of all the famous names that visited this great civilization seeking knowledge and wisdom," said Frankie, as they gazed at a massive granite statue of a man with the head of an Ibis bird.

"Who is that?" asked Chuka, pointing at the smoothed stone artefact.

"That," explained Frankie, gazing up at the giant pen and papyrus paper notepad in the statue's hands, "is Djehuty, the Kemetic god of writing, magic and wisdom. How appropriate that it be here, in this building, with one of the wisest men in history."

All three of them had now stopped and were peering up at the six metre ebony sculpture. Without taking his eyes off the immense idol, Chuka asked,

"You said something about 'famous names' visiting ancient Egypt. Who were they?"

Still admiring the skill and craftsmanship that must have gone into the fantastic figure, Frankie answered. "Actually, when I said 'visited', I really meant 'stayed' and when I say 'stayed', I really mean 'studied'. Now where to start...It's a *really* long list. I'll start by telling you something the philosopher St. Clement of Alexandria once said. He said that 'if you were to write a book of one-thousand pages, you would not be able to put down the names of all the Greeks who went to the Nile Valley in ancient Egypt to study, and even those who did not go, claimed that they did, because it was so prestigious.' That being said, I will try to summarise for you."

"Aristotle came to study philosophy for thirteen years in Kemet in 300BC and Pythagoras studied mathematics in Kemet for twenty-two years in 535BC under the tutelage of the Arch-Prophet Sonches. Hippocrates studied medicine in Kemet for twenty years. Socrates also studied in Kemet in his youth for around fifteen years. Plato studied philosophy at the Temple of Waset in Kemet for thirteen years under

Sechnuphis of Heliopolis. Euclid studied in Kemet for eleven years. Archimedes studied engineering in Kemet in 270BC. Not to mention Herodotus, Diodorus, Thales, Euripides, Lycurgus the Spartan, Solon the Athenian, Eudoxos...the list goes on and on. They all came to study in Kemet, because it was the intellectual centre of the ancient world."

"It may therefore not come as a surprise to you that Black Africans had already mastered the fields of the arts and sciences thousands of years before any Europeans arrived. Imhotep himself is testament to that. But let's look at, say, Philosophy - something that numerous Greeks came to Kemet to study. Whose ancient writings did the Greeks learn from? There are several possibilities: Imhotep himself, Ptahhotep, Amenemhat, Merikare, Duauf, Amenhotep, Akhenaten, Kagemni, Akhethotep, Sehotepibre...again, the list goes on and on, although many other names have been lost to history. These men and many others were studying and practising philosophy, thousands of years prior to the Greeks arrival in 700BC. It should also be noted that it is highly likely that they were well versed in other subjects such as mathematics, science and engineering because the Kemetu did not consider science and philosophy as separate subjects to be studied. They understood that everything is connected. That they are all part of the same connected universe," concluded Frankie.

"Wow! Even *I* didn't know all that!" exclaimed Zabrina.

"I didn't know *any* of that," confessed the gobsmacked kid.

"You'd be surprised just how many people don't know any of that either," said Frankie. "Anyway, it's been about half an hour. I think it's time to look in on our resident genius. I'm talking about *Imhotep* by the way, not you." smiled Frankie, looking in Chuka's direction.

Returning to Imhotep and his colleagues, Chuka and Zabrina were shocked to find them all fast asleep.

"No, no, no!" wailed Chuka, rushing over to the banquet table.

"But this doesn't make any sense," complained Zabrina, standing over the slumbering sages. "There was enough refined sugar in those biscuits to bring an Egyptian mummy back to life!"

Just then, the men began to rouse from their nap.

"Not sure what happened there," said one of them, as they all looked at each other. "Anyway, let's get back to work on the...on the...pyramid. That's the word I was looking for. Let's get back to work on the pyramid."

On their way back to their work table, the other man commented, "Yes. If we don't get it completed in time, King...King...What's his name?"

"King Djoser," stated the first man, helping out his forgetful friend.

"Yes. Thank you. King Djoser will not be best pleased."

As they returned to their work table and began looking over the pyramid plans, Imhotep asked, "What was I saying again?" The two other men looked at each other with wide eyes, as if they had never heard him utter those words before. The reason they did so, was because *they had never heard him utter those words before.*

"What on earth is going on here?" asked the first man, worry etched on his face like the hieroglyphs on the walls of the temple.

"I'm not really sure," replied Imhotep. "Perhaps we are under-nourished. Let's all have something to eat."

"Excellent idea, Imhotep," declared the second man, as the three architects returned to the banquet table to resume consuming the calorific confectioneries.

This sequence of devouring desserts and misplaced memories continued, unabated for several days until King Djoser, unhappy at the lack of progress on his pyramid, summoned the men to his palace.

Chuka and chums followed Imhotep and his colleagues, as they were escorted to the Pharaoh's residence by the palace guards. The looks on the men's faces were a mixture of fear and 'fogginess', as if they knew that they *should* be afraid, but they couldn't quite remember exactly *why* they should be afraid.

"I can't help but feel partly responsible for this situation," confessed Chuka.

"Partly responsible?" laughed Frankie. We are all *fully* responsible for this situation."

"What did *I* do?" asked Zabrina, as the group made its way through the sunny city streets, packed with people staring and wondering what was happening.

"Together, we have reduced perhaps the keenest intellect in the *world* to something that probably wouldn't even be the keenest intellect in a *goldfish bowl*," bemoaned Frankie, watching the crowds bowing to Imhotep in reverence, as he walked through their neighbourhoods.

"I think you may be exaggerating the point slightly," said Chuka.

"I agree," said Zabrina. "Besides, what's the worst thing that could happen to these guys? Mmm? I bet all they get is a 'slap on the wrist', nothing more."

"You think so? Tell me," responded Frankie with a grin, "what's your record on bets recently?"

Arriving at Pharaoh Djoser's royal palace, the group were met by a wall of decorated cylindrical columns that seemed to reach all the way up into the sky. Two guards, dressed in attire even more sumptuous than the first, took over and escorted the party of six up the seemingly endless stone staircase and into the building. This palace was even more lavishly decorated than Imhotep's residence. There were cylindrical column after cylindrical column for as far as the eye could see. All were decorated in multi-coloured engravings, depicting gods, previous kings and of course, the current King - Djoser. Surrounding these images were hundreds of hieroglyphs all in vibrant green, gold and red.

As the company walked through the palace hall, all the King's men and all the King's women bowed to Imhotep, paying homage to his brilliance. Finally, after what seemed to last an age, they arrived at Pharaoh Djoser's throne room. Everyone bowed as they entered the royal chamber, including Imhotep.

"Why are *we* bowing?" asked Zabrina, her eyes still facing the floor.

"I have no idea," replied Frankie, looking up in her direction.

"Me neither," admitted Chuka, standing up. "It just seemed the right thing to do. I mean, look at this place. Look at *him*."

Our three futuristic-friends could easily be forgiven for doing so, as the royal chamber coupled with the King himself, was probably the grandest setting any of them had ever found themselves in.

The design of the throne room mirrored the palace almost exactly, except that absolutely everything was gold. The floor, the walls, the ceiling, the columns, the curtains, the statues, the steps leading up to the throne, the King's clothing, everything. Even the King's skin was covered in golden glitter make-up. What you could see underneath all the gold he was wearing. Snapping out of her trance just in time, Frankie noticed King Djoser rise off his royal rear, walk down the steps, put his arm around Imhotep and take him to a private section of the throne room. Chuka and friends quickly darted into the room after them.

They found themselves in what could be called a parlour. It was a much more casual setting than the main chamber, with soft furnishings and several rugs spread across the floor. The King took of his crown, sat down on a soft leather bound chair and gestured to Imhotep to do the same.

"Imhotep. My Adviser, my friend. You look awful. What is the matter?" he asked leaning forward in his chair.

"My King," replied Imhotep, before taking a deep exhausted breath. "I thank you for your concern. As you can imagine, as your Chief Physician, I have already taken steps to self-diagnose."

"And what have you learnt?"

"My King, I have a condition of excess sugar in my body. This is causing me great exhaustion, loss of memory and I am unable to concentrate. As a result it is affecting my reasoning and my ability to make accurate calculations. In short, I am no longer fit to serve as your adviser." Imhotep fell to his knees. "I have failed you my King! Please forgive me!"

Helping his trusted ally to his feet, the Pharaoh said, "There is nothing to forgive. You are the 'Great Imhotep'! You could never fail me. You will cure yourself."

"My Lord, I have tried. I restricted my diet to only vegetables, nuts and water. Yet my urine continues to smell sweet, I am still forgetful and I remain exhausted."

"Fear not Imhotep. We shall implore the goddess Sekmet to deliver you from this illness. All will be well. Do not worry," announced Pharaoh Djoser, placing his hands on his friend's shoulders.

"Alright people, I think we've seen enough," observed Frankie, pausing the flow of time with a wave of her hand. "And Imhotep has *definitely* had enough, don't you think?"

One look at the despairing declared demigod and both Chuka and Zabrina were in full agreement with Frankie.

"Yeah, it's definitely time to call it quits on this experiment," admitted Chuka.

"I agree. Let's put an end to this," conceded Zabrina.

And with that, they all found themselves back at the entrance to Imhotep's temple gazing across the river Nile once again.

"Well that was a bust, wasn't it? What's an Arusi got to do to get a break around here?" groaned Zabrina, pacing back and forth.

"What about me?" moaned Chuka, watching Zabrina. "I'm down two-zero and about to lose my

129

lovely lollipop-licking lifestyle. What do you stand to lose?"

"Well, my reputation for one. And two, this one, will never, ever let me live it down," responded Zabrina, pointing at Frankie.

"She's right, you know," confirmed Frankie, with a cheeky grin. "But in all seriousness, you guys *are* down two-zero. Do you wish to concede defeat now...?"

"Never!" cut in Zabrina, halting her pacing to raise a chocolate fist of determination. "We'll never give up. We're in this to the bitter end."

"From the way things are going so far, I think the end *will* be bitter for me, very bitter indeed. It definitely *won't* be sweet, I can tell you that for nothing!" grumbled Chuka, with a furrowed brow.

"We're not done *just* yet," encouraged Zabrina, looking him square in the eyes and placing a huge 'choccy-biccy' hand on his shoulder. "We just need to win at *one* of the tasks to win the whole thing. Remember?"

Chuka nodded with a faint look of recollection on his face.

"So all we need to do is win the *next* task!" explained Zabrina, with as much enthusiasm as she could muster.

"I guess," sighed Chuka, with as much enthusiasm as *he* could muster - which wasn't much.

"She's right. All you guys need to do is win the final task and you *will* win the whole thing," clarified Frankie, with as much enthusiasm as *she* could muster – which wasn't much either. "But before we move on to the final task, let's see how history would have looked if we'd allowed this scenario to play out."

Imhotep's temple and the entire city vanished and they found themselves in the parlour of Chuka's house in Owerri.

"Hurray. I'm home!" he yelled, diving onto the family sofa. "Does that mean that all bets are off and I can go back to my sweet, sweet life?" he asked, giving one of the sofa cushions a hug.

"I'm afraid not, because although this *is* your home in *space,* it is *not* your home in *time*," replied Frankie, looking around the room.

"W-h-a-t?" bawled the bewildered boy, before covering his face with the cushion.

"I think I understand," remarked Zabrina. "We're in Chuka's house in the timeline where Imhotep didn't design the world's first pyramid. Correct?"

"Give that Arusi a chocolate cigar!" cried Frankie, clapping her hands.

"Okay," said Chuka, tossing the cushion aside, standing up and pointing to Zabrina whilst addressing Frankie. "You mentioned the word 'timeline', Zabrina. So what's the date, Frankie?"

"Couldn't tell you I'm afraid," said Frankie, shrugging. "Because Imhotep's intellect was never fully utilised, Kemet never went on to be the greatest civilisation the world has ever seen, so their inventions were never discovered and copied by other civilisations all over the world. So no three-hundred and sixty-five day calendar. I couldn't tell you the time either, because nobody discovered and copied the clocks they invented."

"I didn't know they invented the calendar and clocks," remarked Chuka. "That's so cool. Let me jot this down because I'm bound to forget," he continued, looking for a pen and paper in a desk.

"I'm afraid you won't find anything in there, my boy. Sadly in this timeline, your Kemetic cousins' inventions of ink, paper and writing itself, weren't discovered and copied either. Not to mention science, philosophy, psychology, what you would call 'religion', engineering, the formula for 'Pi', ocean navigation, maths, geometry, architecture, farming, the ox-drawn plough and sickle, canals and irrigation, astronomy, medicine, surgery, surgical instruments, metallurgy, glass making, furniture, toothpaste, the lever or 'shadoof'...the list just goes on and on." Frankie sighed and then paused for a moment, before concluding with: "Imagine that. An entire civilisation not reaching its full potential because one man ate too much junk food. Tragic, isn't it?"

"What is *really* tragic is how much you're flogging your point," remarked Zabrina. "We get it. Don't we Chuka?"

The 'schooled' school-boy nodded faintly, as he pondered Frankie's poignant points.

"Come on Chuka! Focus!" commanded Zabrina, tapping him on the shoulder. "We've got one more chance to win this thing and I, for one, believe we can do it. What do you say?!"

Chuka looked up from the floor and sighed. Then, spying something out of the corner of his eye, he said. "Just give me a minute, will you?" And he slowly made his way to the kitchen.

After a few moments, Frankie called out to him. "You won't find anything in there chum."

Chuka came out of the kitchen, throwing sweet wrappers on the floor. "Is this some kind of sick joke?! I opened about ten bars of chocolate and they were all empty! Don't tell me the ancient Egyptians invented chocolate too?"

"Actually, no. That was the Mayans, I believe," responded Frankie. "Sorry about that, but as I said at the beginning, this isn't really your house and those weren't really chocolate bars. Besides you're not really hungry. It's just force of habit. You're still at your grandparents' house. Remember?"

"Yeah, I know," groaned Chuka. "I still think it was a cheap trick. Come on. Let's just get on with the last task."

"That's the spirit!" yelled Zabrina.

"Okay. I'm ready to go. Where, or should I say, *when* to this time?" asked Chuka.

"You really *are* getting the hang of this," praised Frankie, with a smile. "As to the question of *where*, as ever we will be remaining in the great continent of Africa. With regards to *when*, how does 140,000BC grab you?"

"140,000BC?" repeated Chuka. "Are we going to feed donuts to dinosaurs?!"

Zabrina slapped her fizzy forehead in disbelief, almost knocking it off her body. "You're only off by about sixty-five million years, kid."

"Hey. Frankie's the historian here, not me," responded Chuka, crossing his arms across his chest.

Frankie chuckled as, for the final time, she transported the trio back through the ages.

Chapter Nine - San, Sun, Sugar, Stamina And Homo Sapiens

The clear deep-blue sky was the perfect backdrop for the glaring yellow sun. Chuka shielded his eyes from its brilliance, as they arrived in the dry savannah grass, which stood up to a metre high from the ground. Taking in a three hundred and sixty degree view of his surroundings and finding grasslands in all directions as far as the eye could see, Chuka asked, "So where are we this time?"

Gazing off into the distance, Frankie replied "We're in Southern Africa and we're here to find the most ancient, still surviving, group of people in the world today. The San people of the Kalahari."

"Are you sure we're in the right place?" asked Zabrina, surveying the setting. "I can't see any sign of a settlement nearby."

"Nor should you," replied Frankie. "These are a migratory people who follow the food and the rains, so they don't drain the resources of a particular place for too long. That way, they help to maintain the balance of nature. They did, however, have temporary settlements and I believe I see one yonder," advised Frankie, pointing in a northerly direction. "Come on. Follow me."

Trudging through the grass behind Frankie, Chuka pleaded, "Can you please tell us *now* what the task is this time, so Zabrina and I can start to formulate a plan?"

Without breaking stride or turning to face the two stragglers, Frankie answered. "With pleasure. But in order for you to understand the task, I first need to tell you a bit about the San people. Okay?"

"Would it make a shred of difference if we said that it was *not* okay?" asked Zabrina.

"No. Not really," answered Frankie, swiftly, before beginning her back-story. "The San people are 'hunter-gatherers'. That means they do not breed animals for food or grow crops. Instead they eat over a hundred types of plants by foraging the land and they capture animals using the ancient method of 'persistence or endurance hunting'."

"What's 'persistence hunting'?" asked Chuka, catching up to Frankie.

"Is it basically never giving up on the hunt?" asked Zabrina, scanning for the settlement.

"Kind of," replied Frankie. "Rather than simply shooting an animal from a distance with a bow and arrow or a catapult or some such device, the San hunters chase down the animal over several kilometres in order to wear the animal down, and then they strike it with a spear or arrow when it is literally too tired to run anymore."

"So it's a battle of stamina," concluded Chuka.

"Essentially yes," confirmed Frankie. "We are here to monitor the effects of eating excess amounts of processed sugar and added fat on the hunter's stamina," said Frankie, finally answering Chuka's original question.

"But how is this any different to the Wall of Benin task?" asked Chuka.

At this point Zabrina chimed in, saying: "This time *will* be different. I've finally worked out what to do. Trust me," she remarked, catching up to Chuka and Frankie.

"And exactly what are you going to do?" enquired Chuka.

"It's pretty technical. I'm not sure you'd understand, but trust me it *will* work."

"Now where have I heard those unwarranted words before," said Chuka, looking up to the sky while scratching his chin. "Oh yeah, I remember. *From you*. The last time *and* the time before that." Chuka looked down at the grassy terrain and sighed before looking up at Zabrina. "Fine. It's not like I really have a choice anyway. I can give up *now* and *definitely* lose, or have a snowflake in the Sahara's chance of winning in this task and only *probably* lose."

"What about the third option?" asked Zabrina, before answering her own question. "Succeeding at this task and winning the whole thing? Mmm?" she said, with a smile and a twinkle in her eyes.

"Hang on guys. I see someone," remarked Frankie, stopping in her tracks and pointing them out for her companions. What Frankie had noticed was a group of five San men crouched around a now burnt out campfire. Dressed in animal skin loincloths, they were busy sharpening their spear heads on well-worn stones. "We're in luck. It looks like these guys are preparing for a hunt."

Once they had finished honing their hunting tools, one of the men, who may have been the leader by way of him clearly being the eldest, (his face was far wrinklier than the other four men) tapped the animal skin bag, they all carried over their shoulders, with his fingers. Each man took this as an instruction to reach into their bags and began to eat the fruits, nuts and vegetables they carried therein.

"Look Chuka," said Frankie, pointing at the food. "Even way back in 140,000BC people were making sure they got their five-a-day. If it's good enough for the world's oldest, still surviving peoples, then it's good enough for you."

Chuka could only purse his lips in response as he was unable to come up with a suitable contradictory reply.

Taking the fact that the men were eating as her cue, Zabrina leapt into action. "Don't you worry Chuka. I know what I'm doing," she proclaimed, as she, for the third and final time, magically remade their berries into buns, their nuts into nougat, their tubers into treacle and their melons into marshmallows.

Within moments of masticating the manufactured morsels, the men reared up abruptly and began scouring the landscape, like a mob of meerkats on the lookout for predators. Without warning, the wrinkly-faced man picked up his spear and sped off running at great speed in an easterly direction. The four other men immediately followed him at a similar pace, spears in hand and bags over their shoulders.

"Come on guys," called Zabrina, chasing after the hunters. "Keep up. This is it!"

Before long, Chuka was way behind the leading pack. Frankie, observing the lagging lad, magically transported him to the spot where the men and Zabrina had now stopped and were hiding behind some bushes.

"Why have they stopped?" asked Frankie, crouching down behind the bushes with Zabrina and Chuka.

"More importantly, why are we hiding behind this bush?" questioned Chuka, standing up and looking in the same direction as the men.

The men had spotted a small herd of antelope some twenty metres away from them. The wrinkly-faced man picked up a handful of sand and let it drop to the ground. The gentle breeze blew the sand in the opposite direction of the antelope's position. He smiled.

He used hand gestures to indicate where he wanted the other four men to go. And then they were off again. Their leader ran directly at the antelope sending them scattering in all directions while the other men flanked the herd, on the left and on the right, and funnelled them back into his path. He selected one of the larger antelope from the herd and the other four men joined him in the chase.

Their leader 'took point' at first, with the others running behind him in single file. In order to keep up with these marathon men, Frankie had conjured up some transport in the shape of a canoe-sized magical watermelon. Inside which, she carved out two seats for her and Chuka. The soft melon flesh provided a wonderful cooling effect on Chuka's back and bottom as they floated, as if on a cushion of air, next to runners.

"Why didn't you do this before?!" called out Chuka enthusiastically. "This is brilliant!"

"It just came to me!" yelled Frankie, the warm air bouncing off their faces as they glided across the savannah.

Zabrina took a different approach. She strapped peppermint sweet-powered cola bottles to her candy cane feet. The resulting bubble bonanza whisking her speedily alongside the men as they hurriedly hunted the hapless herbivore.

After about an hour of running, Frankie and Chuka were expecting to see the usual 'sugar crash' and the men begin to slow down and fall off the pace, similar to what happened in ancient Benin. But that didn't happen. The men, changing their positions every fifteen minutes or so, kept pace with the antelope, who were still about twenty metres away from them.

"I don't believe it," remarked Chuka. "It's actually working. I'm actually going to win. I can almost taste that crunchy chin-chin."

"Actually that's a cricket you can taste," remarked Frankie, noticing a tiny leg protruding from the corner of Chuka's mouth.

"Eurgh!" he grimaced, spitting out the irritating insect.

"You *always* keep your mouth closed when flying at speed in a magic watermelon, in the middle of the South African flatlands, while chasing San hunters. I thought everyone knew that," said Frankie, with a wink. "Still, this isn't exactly what I'd come to expect of these experiments. Those guys should be on their last legs about now, what with all the processed sugar they ate. What's going on?" petitioned a puzzled Frankie, scratching her pineapple chin with her little palm fruit finger. "Wait a minute...sniff...sniff," snorted Frankie, sampling the air and looking around. "I smell sorcery."

"Hang on," responded Chuka. "You can 'smell sorcery'? How is that even possible? You don't even have a nose."

"You're absolutely right. I *don't* have a nose," confirmed Frankie, feeling the front of her fruity face with her fibrous fingers. "But I do 'knows' when someone is manufacturing mischief by meddling with magic."

"Well don't look at me. That's your thing, not mine. The only other person who could do that is..."

Chuka and Frankie looked at each other and then at Zabrina, who, along with the pack-hunting predators, had almost caught up with the sapped steenbok.

Frankie held high her 'horticultured' hands and once again the hour halted for everyone except her, Chuka and Zabrina.

Realising what had happened, Zabrina called out to Frankie. "Hey! What're you doing?"

"What are *you* doing?" asked Frankie, floating over on the melon boat to Zabrina, between the now 'frozen' hungry-hunters and their potential prey.

"I'm about to win the bet, that's what *I'm* doing," responded Zabrina. "Is that why you paused time at the moment of my victory? Mmm? To stop me from winning? That's really low. Isn't it Chuka?"

"Err, yeah. It would be," said Chuka. "Except for-"

"Except for what?" demanded Zabrina, her gaze flicking back and forth between Chuka and Frankie.

"Except for the fact that I suspect that someone is manipulating this moment with maleficent magic," said Frankie, staring at Zabrina.

"What? You think I've been using magic to change the outcome of the experiment! How dare you! I've *never* been so insulted in all my existence!" yelled Zabrina, shaking her cola-can arms in the air with such vigour that they started to bulge.

"Really? *Never*?" asked Frankie, with a cheeky grin on her fructose and fibre face. "Anyway, I haven't *actually* accused you of anything yet. I said that I *suspected* that someone was using magic to alter the outcome of this experiment," said Frankie, defending her corner.

"Yeah...but...I mean, who else here knows magic, except for you and Zabrina? It's kind of obvious *who* you suspect. Isn't it, Frankie?" pointed out Chuka.

"Yeah!" cried an affronted Zabrina, turning her back on the pair.

"Okay. Yes. I do suspect you. Of course I suspect you! You had the means, the opportunity, the motive *and* you're the only person within a hundred miles, apart from me, who can perform magic!" shouted Frankie.

"Did it ever occur to you that the 'magic', as you call it, is being performed by none other than these amazing athletes with their excellent examples of endurance? Mmm?" suggested Zabrina, gesturing to the five San tribesmen, who were all fixed in a different positions of mid-stride.

Frankie stared at Zabrina for a few seconds before responding. "Are you asking me if I think that these five men, 'excellent examples of endurance' they may be, are able to change the fundamental laws of human biology? Is that your question? Mmm. Let me think about that for a few minutes. No!"

"Look ladies, can we just call it a draw?" asked Chuka, attempting to calm things down.

"No. We can't. A draw means we still lose overall," explained Zabrina.

"Okay, okay. I know how to settle this," said Frankie.

"Oh yeah? How?" questioned Zabrina.

"Well, as you know, we Arusi are a bit old-fashioned when it comes to magic. We need to gesture with our hands in order to cast spells. So I just need to keep an eye on your hands to make sure they're not involved in any sneaky spell casting during the experiment."

"Fine with me," replied Zabrina, with a shrug.

"Great. I'm going to 'rewind' the hunt to the midway point, and all three of us will travel together in the magic melon, so I can keep a close eye on you," said Frankie, her eyes fixed on Zabrina's hands.

Once the hunt resumed, as expected the men soon began to tire, their bodies beginning to slump as their pace began to slow down. But suddenly all five men jerked upwards as if standing to attention in a military parade, and resumed their earlier speed. Zabrina's honeyed hands, which she held in front of herself, were both unmoved. Frankie could, however, still identify the unmistakable scent of sorcery. Frankie looked all around for the origin of the enchantment until, much to her surprise and disgust, she located it.

Incredibly, Zabrina had 'grown' another 'hand', from of all places, her bottom.

"Oh...my...gosh!" yelled Frankie, as she caught sight of the four chocolate fingers poking out from Zabrina's backside.

"What is it?" asked Chuka, turning to see what Frankie was looking at.

"Oh...my...days!" cried the amazed adolescent, as he caught sight of the posterior protruding pinkies. Or rather, the bum bulging brownies. "I really hope that *is* what I think it is and *not* what it looks like!" he said, his face screwed up like a prune at the image, which was now seared into his brain forever.

"Zabrina. Care to explain this?" asked Frankie.

"Explain what?" asked Zabrina turning to see what Frankie and Chuka were looking at.
"Oh...ah...that...mmm...well..." Zabrina paused for a moment before letting out a quiet sigh and finally saying: "Alright, fine! It *was* me! *I* was magically meddling with the marathon men!" she confessed, withdrawing the chocolate fingers back whence they came, like snails retreating back into their shells.

"Looks like we caught you 'red-handed' or should I say 'brown-handed?' " laughed Frankie, bringing the hunt to a halt.

"Thanks a lot Zabrina," cried Chuka. "I'm never going to be able to look at chocolate fingers in the same way ever again because of you! In fact I'm never going to be able to look at *any* sweets, biscuits or cakes in the same way ever again, now that we've definitely lost the bet!" lamented the licked lad. Chuka sighed. "I never really stood a chance of winning. Did I guys?"

"Not really," admitted Frankie, who, looking at Chuka's depressed demeanour, now had mixed feelings about winning the bet.

"Sorry kid. I did my best. I truly did," responded the down-hearted and defeated demigod.

"So what now?" questioned Chuka. "Back to my grandparents' house, I presume?"

"Well, yes. The experiment is complete. You've seen for yourself the harmful effects of not eating fruits, nuts and vegetables, or as you humans put it, 'not getting your five-a-day'. You know that eating too much processed sugar and added fat seriously damages your body and your brain. And that it *does* actually stop you from reaching your full potential in life," explained a very serious looking Frankie, to an even more serious looking Chuka.

"Can we go now?" asked Zabrina, climbing out of the watermelon carriage.

Frankie nodded, smiling at her, almost apologetically, as she ended the illusion.

Once again, Chuka was back at his grandparents' house, sitting on his bed, being hugged by his grandma and being told-off by his grandad. But he didn't mind the 'telling-off', he was just happy to be back.

Then, quite unexpectedly, his grandparents simply faded away.

"What's going on?!" cried Chuka, attempting to hold on to their disappearing bodies. "Frankie?! Zabrina?! What's happening?!"

But Frankie was nowhere to be seen. Neither was Zabrina. Had they also faded away or had they simply gone, now that the bet was over? With this question and the mystery of what had happened to his grandparents turning over in his mind, he rushed around the house, checking every room and calling for them as he did so. He was the only person left in the house.

Chuka ran out into the compound, shouting their names as he scoured his surroundings. Still calling for them, he ran out into the street. Spotting Chinedu in the distance, he yelled his name and ran to meet him. The closer he got, the blurrier Chinedu appeared, until he vanished too.

Every time Chuka tried to speak to one of the villagers, the same thing happened. Eventually, he fell to his knees, held his face in his hands and began to cry. Seeing his tears literally falling through him and onto the brown earth, Chuka realised that he, too, was disappearing.

"Frankie!!!..."

In flash, Chuka was back in Southern Africa at the moment just before he first encountered the five San hunters. Frankie and Zabrina were there too.

"What...was...that!?" yelled the youngster breathlessly, tears streaming down his face.

"That," Frankie responded, "was the end result of the San people eating too much junk food and not getting their five-a-day. Because they no longer had the required stamina to hunt, they couldn't continue their way of life and they ended up descending into despair, disease and self-destruction." Frankie took a moment to look all around her, before continuing. "They all died out. And as a result, millions of their descendants were never born. Your ancestors Chuka. And the ancestors of billions of other African women and men. They never existed, so your grandparents never existed, your parents never existed and therefore *you* never existed. All those people who were never even born, so could never reach their full potential and all because their ancient ancestors' bellies were full of sweets, cakes and biscuits."

"It wasn't my idea by the way," commented Zabrina, giving Frankie a scornful look.

"I'm sorry for the stress that caused you," said Frankie. "As I'm sure you've guessed by now, none of it was real. Your grandparents, Chinedu, the villagers - they're all fine. I showed you all that, so you would have a truly personal understanding of the consequences of living an unhealthy lifestyle."

"And you think *that* was the best way to do it?" said the still simmering child, wiping the tears from his eyes.

"Will you ever forget this?" asked Frankie.

"Never," replied Chuka, through gritted teeth.

"Then it was the best way."

Chapter Ten - Taste, Twists, Temptation And Truths

"I don't know exactly, but I believe they're here to show you some truths about life and the future. *Your* life, *your* future and the limitless possibilities of it all," replied grandpa Kelechi, with conviction.

On hearing those assured words spoken in that familiar tone, Chuka slowly pulled his face away from under grandma Nneka's patented, 'under-the-chin hug'. Being greeted by the completely opaque sight of his grandparents, he hugged his grandma even harder.

"Oh. Don't worry child. You're safe with us. We won't let anything bad happen to you. Will we husband?" she said, rubbing his back gently.

"Of course not," agreed grandpa Kelechi.

With a broad smile across his face, Chuka gave his grandfather a big hug too. "It's so good to see you guys again!"

"Again?" Since when?" asked grandma Nneka.

Chuka told his grandparents all about his adventures with the Arusi. For several moments after he had finished telling his tale, they were both speechless, which was a pretty amazing feat for grandpa Kelechi, who was rarely lost for words.

As expected though, he was the first to respond to his grandson's exciting escapade. "I knew the Arusi were here to give you some guidance boy, but that is just...incredible!"

"I understand all that, but tricking you into thinking that we all just vanished into thin air - I can't say I believe that was necessary. In fact, it was totally uncalled for in my opinion," lambasted grandma Nneka, reaching out to him. "Are you sure you're ok?" she asked, holding his hands.

"I am now that everything's back to normal," replied Chuka, squeezing his gran's hands tightly.

"Well not quite *everything's* back to normal," corrected grandpa.

"Oh no!" cried Chuka, looking around the room, frantically. "What's different? Did we do something in the past that's changed the present? Tell me-"

"Calm down my boy, calm down. Nothing *here* has changed," replied grandpa. "I meant that *you* have changed or at least you're *going* to. Because, from what you said, you lost the bet. Right?"

"Right..." said Chuka, with a relaxed sigh. "...I *did* lose the bet and I *will* change. Starting today. I agree with grandma that 'the disappearing act' trick they played on me was way over the top. But it definitely made me think very seriously about how my unhealthy lifestyle affects, not just myself but, my family and friends too."

Standing up with his hands on his hips like a superhero, Chuka announced: "From now on, I will eat mostly healthy foods and I will do more exercise to help me achieve my full potential in life!"

"Glad to hear it, Chuks," said grandpa. "It won't be easy, but your family will support you all the way. You know, I've been reading up on this," he continued, taking a small notepad out of his shirt pocket and putting on his reading glasses. "Did you know that because of its addictive nature, refined sugar is no different to any other drug and it enters the bloodstream in the same way as caffeine, alcohol and nicotine? Did you know that over consumption of processed sugar leads to memory problems, 'brain fog', anxiety, depression, insomnia, it can suppress your immune system and it can reduce concentration levels - like at school for example. It can even lead to dementia and Type 2 diabetes. We just want to protect you from all of that."

Cupping his face in her hands and giving him one of her proudest smiles, grandma Nneka added: "We'll take small steps to begin with. Okay? Don't try and run before you can walk."

"I get it. I truly get it, thanks to Frankie and now you guys. I *am* going to make this change and I know I can rely on you guys to help me foster the discipline I need to succeed."

On hearing those words, grandpa Kelechi leapt to his feet. "Discipline? That's my favourite word! You're definitely in the right place and with the right people to succeed in this endeavour…Actually, unbeknownst to you, your grandma and I have *already* been supporting you in your quest to achieve a healthier lifestyle."

"Huh? How?"

Grandpa Kelechi nodded an instruction to his wife.

"I'll be back in a minute," she said, exiting the room, only to return moments later holding a bowl with a couple of biscuits in it.

As she laid the bowl on the bedroom table, Chuka immediately recognised them as the ones she secretly smuggled to him a couple of days ago, completely against grandpa Kelechi's express wishes. Chuka went into complete panic mode.

"What are those? I've never seen those before in my entire life! And who are you? Actually, where am I? How did I get here? This isn't my house! Err...I want my mummy!"

Seeing that his grandson was about to blow a fuse, grandpa Kelechi quickly stepped in. "It's alright. I already know about the treats your grandma has been sneaking to you."

"You - you do?" replied Chuka.

"Guess what though?" said grandpa Kelechi, with a cheeky grin.

"W-h-a-t?" asked Chuka, not sure what to expect.

"They weren't really shop-bought. They were made by your grandma's fair hands from produce grown on our very own farm," confessed the boy's grandfather.

"So you knew all along?" asked Chuka.

Grandpa Kelechi nodded.

Sitting on his bed, Chuka addressed his grandma, "I should have known really. You and grandpa have always been a great team. You would never go behind his back in anything. Would you?"

Grandma Nneka shook her head as she smiled at her husband. "You're not upset?"

"Upset? No. Relieved more like and...well, curious. How on earth did you manage to make them soooo delicious?"

"Simple really," she answered. "I used naturally sweet ingredients like pineapple, mango and banana instead of processed sugar. That way you get the naturally occurring fructose, *as well as* the vitamins and minerals. You also get the fibre from the fresh fruit, which helps to fill you up because it takes longer to digest. And because the food takes longer to digest, the sugar is released into your body gradually, giving you a more stable supply of energy."

"So no more 'sugar crashes' which can make you moody and irritable," added grandpa.

"Come on," said grandma, gesturing to her husband. "Let's leave the boy to get ready for breakfast." And with that, they exited the bedroom, leaving Chuka feeling both exhilarated and nervous at the thought of the monumental change that was ahead of him.

The sound of someone knocking on his door interrupted Chuka's contradictory contemplations.

"I'm okay. Really, I-" He started to say, opening the door to reveal Frankie and Zabrina.

"Hi. Can we come in? We thought it might be a little rude if we just appeared in your room like last time," Zabrina explained.

"Sure. You've come to make sure I keep my end of our bargain, haven't you?" asked the young man, closing the door behind them.

"Not at all," replied Zabrina. "We've just come to say goodbye."

"*And* to make sure that you're okay," added Frankie.

"As I was about to say to my grandparents, before I realised it was you guys. I'm good. I truly understand how a person's eating habits and lifestyle can have a massive impact on what they go on to achieve in their lives."

"Oh. How so?" enquired Frankie, crossing her arms.

"Well, having seen all the achievements that could have been lost to mankind simply because of bad diet, it makes me wonder what achievements I may lose out on because of *my* unhealthy lifestyle."

"Go on," encouraged Frankie.

"So I'm going to try my very best to live a healthy lifestyle, so that something as basic as eating too much junk food, doesn't stop me from, to use your words Frankie, 'reaching my full potential'."

"Hoot!" Frankie blew her non-existent nose into a handkerchief as the tears rolled down her fruity face. "My little boy's all grown up."

"Tears? Really?" commented a far from empathetic Zabrina, her face wrought with contempt.

"It's okay," said Chuka, walking over to Frankie. "Though I *still* don't get how you can smell stuff *and* blow your nose without actually *having* a nose" he chuckled.

"It's all a bit technical," sniffed Frankie.

"…Magic," they said together.

The pair hugged. One in gratitude and the other with pride. As they separated, some of Frankie's tears wiped off onto Chuka's face. It felt sticky and smelt sweet.

"Pineapple juice?" he asked with a smile.

"Yeah. Sorry," Frankie smiled back, tossing him her handkerchief. But the piece of white cotton never reached its destination, as suddenly, it was halted in mid-flight.

"Sorry, but I'm getting a little fed-up with all this 'lovey-dovey' stuff!" barked Zabrina. "So you won the bet! There's no need to rub my face in it!"

"Who's rubbing your face in it?" I'm just happy for the lad, that's all. Anyway, that's no reason to freeze time," complained Frankie, raising her hand, as she prepared to put paid to Zabrina's pause.

"Hold up," requested Zabrina, grabbing Frankie's hand just before she could snap her fructose fingers and return the flow of time along its steady course. "*I* have a wager for *you* this time."

"A wager for me? What's the catch?" asked Frankie. "Anyway, you already lost and I really don't want to put Chuka through any more tasks. I think he's pretty much had his fill. Don't you?"

"Yeah, I know, I know. But this would be just between you and me. Chuka never needs to know about it. Besides don't you think it's only fair that *I* get a chance to set at least *one* task."

"I...guess..." replied Frankie, lowering her hand.

"Look, I get it," stated Zabrina, as she purposefully walked around the motionless young man. "Too much sugar can adversely affect strength, speed, stamina, concentration and memory, but-"

"*Can* affect?" interrupted Frankie.

"Alright, alright. Too much sugar *does* adversely affect strength, speed, stamina, concentration and memory..." corrected Zabrina, licking her chocolate fingers, "...but...mmm...you never once mentioned how great sugar actually *tastes*."

Zabrina tore off a piece of her striped, glazed donut. "I bet that if Chuka tastes just one piece of my glazed donut, he'll toss his grandmother's home-made biscuits in the bin. Which, incidentally, is where I think they belong. I mean, 'healthy treats'? What's next? Drinking water instead of an energy drink when you're thirsty? It's madness!" she moaned.

Noticing the fist-sized hole in Zabrina's bottom-half, Frankie mentioned, "You know it kind of looks as if you just tore that piece of donut out of your bottom."

"I think you'll find that it's my hip," replied Zabrina, gesturing to her lower half.

"Technically you don't have hips," countered Frankie.

"*Technically* I don't have a bottom either," challenged Zabrina.

Frankie's already naturally furrowed forehead furiously furrowed further. "Okay, so you want to carry out one final task. A 'taste test'? Is that it?"

"Exactly," smiled Zabrina, nibbling on the piece of donut. "I propose that we have a 'winner takes all' final bet, with *me* making the rules for once. If Chuka prefers the taste of my donut over his grandmother's biscuits then we never appear to him in the first place and all of this will never have happened."

"But then what happens to Chuka?" asked the inquisitive immortal.

"He continues with his blissfully ignorant existence, just like most humans, I guess," replied the decidedly detached demi-god. "Why? Does it matter?"

"It will matter to *Chuka* and it matters to *me*," revealed Frankie.

"Ani," said Zabrina, calling Frankie by her Arusi name. "You are the god of the earth, morality, fertility and creativity. Over the centuries I have watched you intervene in the lives of *hundreds of thousands* of beings, helping to change their lives time and time again. Why, all of a sudden, are you getting so emotional about *one* individual?"

"I can't quite put my finger on it, Ekwensu," said Frankie, calling Zabrina by *her* Arusi name. "But there is something very special about that human. I believe he will go on to do great things and in doing so he will motivate others to do the same."

"Are you saying that you, a god, are afraid you might lose?" said Zabrina.

"No. That is not what I am saying," responded Frankie. "I'm confident that Chuka will make the right choice. But what's in it for me if I win? Like I said, I've already won, so what's *my* motivation to take this bet?"

"Fine," said Zabrina. "What do you want?"

Frankie walked over to the bedroom window and peered out at the clear, blue morning. A short moment later, she turned back to face her angry Arusi acquaintance and the transfixed teenager.

"Ekwensu, you are the god of bargains, chaos and change. These are powers that can be of service to the child on his new and challenging journey. If I win, you will carry out three requests for Chuka at a time of his choosing."

Zabrina narrowed her eyes. "Requests? What sort of requests?"

"Three simple requests that are well within your power to carry out. That's all," clarified Frankie.

Zabrina smiled. "*Three wishes*? Really? Do I look like a genie to you?"

Frankie ignored Zabrina's remark and offered her hand by way of agreement. "Do we have a deal?" she asked.

It was now Zabrina's turn to consider the content of the curious contract in her carbonated cranium. After a short period of heady effervescent activity, they shook hands and by doing so, created the world's first cinnamon roll, chocolate finger, mango, banana, okra, carrot, ube and palm fruit salad.

Handshake salad still in progress, Zabrina added: "Actually, the more I think about it, to make the 'taste test' a challenge for Chuka, they should be the same kind of food. Right? They should both be biscuits. One home-made and the other bought from a shop."

"I actually agree with that. But we don't have any shop-bought biscuits in the house. His grandfather threw them all away. Remember?" pointed out Frankie.

"That shouldn't be a problem for a time-traveller like you. Just pop back to before grandpa Kelechi threw them away and grab a couple of biscuits from Chuka's stash."

"That's a great idea. I'll be right back," said Frankie, before vanishing and bringing to an end, the historical handshake. And in a couple of seconds, she was back, chocolate biscuits in hand.

"Got them," she declared, placing them on a tissue on the table.

"Everything go okay? Any problems getting them?" enquired Zabrina.

"No problems at all. I simply froze time, as usual, got the stuff and I was away. I did have a look around the house while I was there though. Come to think of it, did I leave that door unlocked?" Frankie asked herself, pointing at the bedroom's internal door.

"What? Who cares? Come on, let's get back in position," remarked Zabrina, as she and Frankie returned to where they were standing when Chuka's animation was suddenly suspended.

Snapping her fingers, Zabrina re-animated the adolescent adventurer. Catching the handkerchief, Chuka wiped Frankie's sweet secretions from his face and hands. Whilst doing so, he noticed the unmistakable sight of his favourite chocolate biscuits on the bedroom table.

"W-what's that doing in here?" he asked, his gaze jumping between Frankie, Zabrina and the baked treats.

"Call it a parting gift," replied Zabrina swiftly, ushering Chuka over to the table where the biscuits lay. "They look good, don't they? Would you like to try one?" she asked, picking up one of the biscuits and offering it to him.

Suddenly, all Chuka could see was a pair of feet with red toenails. Crawling away from them, he almost bumped into a smaller pair of feet with unpainted toenails. Looking to his left, he noticed a shopping bag that had fallen on its side, its contents spilt out onto the kitchen floor. The shiny red and blue packaging of one of the items compelling him to investigate further.

Sitting on the floor next to it, he picked up the packet, sending its contents tumbling out in front of him. The chocolate biscuits were the same colour as the feet he had seen earlier, but the aroma coming from them was much more enticing. He put the sweet smelling disc into his mouth. The refined sugar, additives and preservatives hit his bloodstream with the power of a ten-metre wave crashing on a rocky cliff face. Saliva poured out of his mouth as he began to devour the delicious delicacy.

So engrossed was he in his pleasure that he didn't see the ringed-fingered hands reach down, pull the treat from his hand and lift him up from the kitchen floor until it was too late. Reaching to retrieve his lost lunch, Chuka tried to tell this lady to put him back down on the floor, but the only sound he could make come from his mouth was: "Waaaahhhh!"

"Hello? Are you okay?" asked Frankie, waving her hand in front of his face.

"Huh?" replied Chuka, shaking his head and taking a step back from the biscuits.

"You sort of zoned out there for a moment," remarked Zabrina.

"That was weird," muttered Chuka to himself, as he looked around the room.

"What was weird?" enquired Frankie.

"What? Oh, nothing. So, yeah. What's with the biscuits?" asked Chuka.

"Like I said, they're kind of a leaving present. Go on. Try one," coaxed Zabrina, using her magic to wave the chocolate biscuit in front of Chuka's face like a pendulum.

"You really want me to eat that biscuit, don't you? Why? Have you put a spell on it or something?"

"Of course not. Have I Frankie?" replied Zabrina.

"I can assure you that she hasn't put a spell on those biscuits. And as you know I can smell magic a mile away. That being said, I think Chuka, what with his recent resolutions, would rather have some of his grandmother's home-made biscuits," suggested Frankie, attempting to pull the tempted teenager away from the buoyant 'biccy'.

"You know these are *absolutely* my favourite biscuits ever," commented Chuka, turning back to face the baked bauble.

"Really? What a curious coincidence. What sweet serendipity. Now you simply *must* have a bite," remarked Zabrina, placing the biscuit in the boy's hand.

The movements of everyone in the room appeared to be going in slow motion as Chuka raised his old 'chocolaty chum' to his chops. Watching him, Zabrina's eyes gradually widened and, bit by bit, a smile spread across her face as she slowly nodded with glee. Frankie's eyes also gradually widened, but in shock rather than glee. The smile fading from her face as she shook her head, not wanting to believe what she was seeing.

Chomping and chewing, Chuka's taste buds were once again engulfed in a wave of refined sugar, added fats, additives and preservatives, and once again, found himself back on that kitchen floor. But this time, the shopping bag was upright and he noticed a tiny orange pop bottle with a face peer round the side of one of the kitchen cupboards. As it revealed itself, Chuka gurgled happily at the sight of the brightly coloured mini-donuts that made up its body, the fun-sized chocolate bars arms and the microscopic marzipan fingers. Walking up to the bag on its teeny-weeny candy cane legs, it smiled at Chuka as it pushed the bag over, tore open the shiny red and blue packaging and beckoned him over to it.

"Mit moz moo!" mumbled Chuka, his mouth full of chocolate biscuit, as he pointed at Zabrina.

"I'm sorry? What?" she replied, her contentment converting into confusion.

"It was you!" clarified Chuka, after he had swallowed the biscuit.

"It was me...what?" asked Zabrina.

"It was you that got me hooked on sugary and fatty foods!" accused the angry adolescent.

"What!?" exclaimed Frankie. "What's he talking about, Zabrina!?"

"I have absolutely no idea," assured the Arusi.

"Oh really?" declared the decidedly dubious teen. "So you're saying that you didn't visit me as a baby and encourage me to eat those biscuits over there?!" he interrogated, pointing to the remaining shop-bought chocolate biscuit on the bedroom table.

"Is there any truth to this?!" asked Frankie, staring at Zabrina.

"There is no truth to this whatsoever," re-confirmed Zabrina, crossing her arms.

"Okay. Then you won't mind us all travelling back to my 1st birthday at precisely twenty-five minutes past three in the afternoon? Actually, better make it *twenty-three* minutes past three just to be safe."

"That's a pretty specific set of date and time coordinates you've got there," remarked Frankie.

"I'll say," agreed Zabrina. "How can you be sure that they're correct?"

"I don't know. I just am."

"Okay then. Let's go," said Frankie.

The parlour walls of Chuka's parents' house were covered in glittery red and golden party decorations. A silver helium-filled balloon in the shape of a 'number one' clung to the ceiling. Different sized boxes of colourfully-wrapped gifts were piled high in one of the corners and an almost completely eaten birthday cake was on the low centre table.

"You were right. That's uncanny," remarked Frankie.

"Come on. Let's get to the kitchen," said Chuka, leading the way.

The time on the kitchen wall clock was twenty-four minutes and fifty-nine seconds past three. Baby Chuka was crawling around on the floor while his sister Chinwe, played with a doll. His mother was doing the dishes.

Right on cue, the pocket-sized persuader 'poofed' into the picture.

"Okay. That's me," admitted Zabrina immediately, holding her 'choccy-biccy' hands up.

With that revelation, Chuka and Frankie gave her the sort of look that needed an overnight soak, stain remover *and* bleach to remove.

"In my defence, I genuinely do not remember this. I mean, I'm centuries old. I can't be expected to remember every slightly questionable thing I've ever done. Now, can I?"

"Slightly questionable?!" responded Chuka. "You call getting an infant hooked on junk food, 'slightly questionable'?!"

"Well, if you think about it, it's really no different to all the junk food advertising constantly shown on TV. And, of course, there's the question of parental and personal responsibility. Isn't there?" asked Zabrina.

"You know what, Zabrina does kind of have a valid point...or three," highlighted Frankie.

The seemingly out of character comment caused Chuka to swiftly switch his focus from Zabrina to

Frankie, his angry glare transforming into a look of total astonishment. "You have *got* to be kidding me," remarked the boy.

"I know. I know. That's pretty much what I said to myself right after I heard myself say it. But...just hear me out. Alright?" implored Frankie.

"Awww, look how cute I look with my tiny soda pop head and mini donut body. I could literally just eat me up, but that might be a bit weird," gushed Zabrina, watching her younger, smaller self.

"Really?!" barked Chuka, turning his angry glare back onto her.

"You look cute too," she responded, with a sheepish grin.

"I think we've seen enough," concluded Frankie, and with that, they were back in the bedroom.

Chuka sat on his bed with his head in his hands.

"As I was saying Chuka," continued Frankie, "that meeting between you and Zabrina, significant though it may seem, was just *one* of the hundreds of times when someone has tried to persuade you to eat processed sugary foods."

"What do you mean?" asked Chuka, raising his head from his hands.

"Well, think about it. Growing up, how many other times did you see brightly decorated junk food packaging with cartoon characters on it designed specifically to grab the attention of young children? How many times did you watch a TV advert attempting to do exactly the same thing? Or even a poster on the side of the road or in a supermarket? Millions of children all over the world have been taught from a very early age to desire processed foods."

"So you're saying it's the corporations who make these foods? It's their fault?" asked Chuka.

Taking a deep breath before speaking, Frankie replied: "It's true to say that they bear *some* responsibility. It is also true to say, as Zabrina pointed out, that parents also bear some responsibility. In my opinion, the bulk of the responsibility."

"Surely you're not blaming my parents?" said Chuka.

"Are you alright in there?" asked grandma Nneka, knocking on the bedroom door.

"Yeah, I'm good. Just talking to the Arusi. I'll be out for breakfast in a minute."

"Oh? Really? Can we meet them?" asked grandpa Kelechi, at which point both Frankie and Zabrina vanished.

"Sorry," replied Chuka, looking around the room. "I don't think that's an option. They're...really shy."

"Shame," said grandma Nneka. "Alright. See you at breakfast."

With that statement, Zabrina and Frankie re-appeared.

Frankie continued: "Chuka, no one's actually *blaming* your parents. But what I *am* saying is that, as their child, they had a duty to *make* you eat your fruits, nuts and vegetables. They had a duty to actively *restrict* the amount of processed food you had access to. They had a duty to *limit* how much added sugar and fat you had in your diet."

The anger Chuka felt for Zabrina began to dissipate as the truth of Frankie's words began to register. After a brief moment, he pushed himself up into a standing position and said: "You know what guys? They're *all* to blame. The corporations, my parents, Zabrina - all of them. But only *I* am responsible. *I* am responsible for what I eat. *I* am responsible for what I drink. *I* am responsible for how much exercise I do. *I* am responsible for *my* choices. And this is the first responsible choice I'm going to make."

Chuka gave the remaining shop-bought biscuit to Zabrina. Then he grabbed his grandma's home-made biscuits and gobbled them down greedily. "Mmm, taking responsibility not only feels great, it tastes great too."

"Wait a minute. Are you *seriously* saying that you prefer your grandma's home-made stuff to your all-time favourite food in the world...ever?" challenged Zabrina, jumping out of her marshmallow chair and waving the chocolate biscuit in front of him.

"Yes, I am. Hold on. Is it me or are you shorter than you used to be?" asked Chuka, noticing that he was almost eye to eye with her.

"It isn't you," said Frankie, walking over to Zabrina, whom she now completely towered over. "Zabrina is shrinking because your desire for fatty and sugary foods is shrinking, as you've shown by the choice you just made."

Chuka was now the same height as the disbelieving deity.

"But why, Chuka? For sucrose sake, why?" pleaded Zabrina.

"Well, my former favourites are much sweeter, but they're too sweet. They have a kind of hard, artificial, saccharine-like taste. It's kind of like a heavyweight boxer is trying to pummel my taste buds into submission. But grandma's tastes naturally sweet. It's full of fresh, fragrant, fruity flavours that are gentle on my taste buds."

By now Zabrina was only up to Chuka's waist. In desperation she made one final effort to win Chuka round to her side. All of a sudden processed sweet and savoury junk food started appearing randomly all over the room. Before Chuka knew what was happening, biscuits, cakes, pies, pizzas, donuts, fizzy drinks and chocolate bars were circling around him like planets round the sun. Zabrina, who was now the same size as she was when she met baby Chuka, hopped from one sugary snack to another, lobbing the processed food at his mouth. Chuka just kept his mouth closed and smiled as he and Frankie shook their heads at her in pity. Eventually, seeing that all her efforts were in vain, Zabrina slumped into her now marshmallow-sized, marshmallow chair and sulked.

Realising that his trials and temptations were finally over, Chuka walked over to Zabrina and knelt down in front of her. "You know what Z? We're good. I understand that, technically, you were just doing your job. I mean, somebody's got to do it. Right?"

"That's right," agreed Zabrina, looking up at him, with a faint smile of appreciation.

"And just for the record, it's not like I'm never, ever going to eat junk food again. I'm just going to stop identifying it as food, you know. Stop seeing it as a 'meal'. Instead, I'm going to recognise it for what it really is - an occasional *treat*, no more, and hopefully, much less."

Chuka patted Zabrina on her tiny soda pop head and walked over to Frankie.

"I really can't thank you enough for opening my eyes to all of this. I can't imagine what my future would look like if you didn't come along."

"I can," replied Frankie, with a smile. "And it looks much better than it did when we first met, I can tell you."

"Can you really see my future? Can *I* see my future?"

"No, but you *can create* it. And hearing your words and seeing your actions, I imagine that you will create a great future, not only for yourself but for others too."

"Sounds kind of deep," remarked Chuka.

"It could be, but that depends on you," explained Frankie.

"Are you guys about done?" interjected Zabrina. "Only I have other places I need to be and being this size is kind of embarrassing."

"Yeah, we're just about done Z," replied Frankie, walking over to the diminutive demi-god. "Unless there's something you wanted to ask me, Chuka?"

"Will I see you guys again?" asked the boy. "I mean, how am I supposed to go back to my boring life after magically travelling through time and space with a couple of demi-gods?"

"You may want to keep that part to yourself," advised Zabrina.

Frankie nodded.

"Listen," replied Frankie. "I can guarantee that if you continue to think, speak and act in the way you have over the last hour, your life will be anything but boring. As to whether we'll all meet again? Just remember - anything's possible."

Chapter Eleven - Hello To New Friends

"One corn on the cob,

two ube,

two African walnuts,

an orange

and an odara.

That was a pretty impressive breakfast you had this morning, Chuka. Your ancestors would be proud. I know I am," remarked grandpa Kelechi, as he and his grandson worked on the farm.

Chuka placed the last of the produce on to the cart just as the sun began to peek out from behind the clouds. "Thanks grandad. I know it's only been a few days since the Arusi left and I started leading a healthier lifestyle, but I already feel fitter. I played thirty minutes of football with Chinedu and the guys yesterday. I even scored a goal. I couldn't dream of that a couple of weeks ago," he said, walking down the farm path.

Halfway down the path from the community farm back to the village main road, they met Chinedu on his way to the palm fruit plantation.

"Good morning sir," he said, greeting grandpa Kelechi. "Chuka, are you coming for a kick-about after lunch?"

"Sorry. Today's my last day. My parents are coming to pick me up after lunch," replied Chuka, shaking hands with his friend.

"Aww. That's a shame. We'll miss having you around," said Chinedu, patting Chuka on the arm.

"More like you'll miss 'nutmegging' me all the time," chuckled Chuka.

"Come on. I didn't 'meg' you *all* the time," replied the lanky lad as the boys laughed.

"Well, you were much more fun on this visit than all the other visits put together," declared Chinedu.

"That's because I *had* so much more fun on this trip than all the other trips put together. No offence grandpa," he quickly added, turning to his grandad.

"None taken, my boy. None taken," he replied, grinning and patting his grandson on the back.

After the two teenagers had finished saying their goodbyes, Chuka and his grandpa continued on their way home.

"Grandpa?" said Chuka, his gaze fixated on the cart full of fruit and vegetables he was pushing.

"Yes Chuka," he replied, at the same time waving to one of his friends sitting on their veranda as they passed his compound.

"I really have enjoyed my visit. I know it began on a bit of a sour note..."

"Or a *sweet* note, depending on how you look at it," smiled grandpa Kelechi.

"Yeah, I guess..." mumbled the embarrassed boy. "But my adventures with the Arusi really gave me so much to think about. And not just about living a healthy lifestyle, but also about African history too. I can't believe they don't teach us anything about the Kemetic Civilisation or The Kingdom of Benin in school," remarked the saddened schoolboy.

"Not to mention...

the Great Zimbabwe Empire,

the Kingdom of Aksum,

the Ethiopian Empire,

the Kingdom of Ghana,

the Mali Empire,

the Kingdom of Kush,

the Songhai Empire,

the Land of Punt,

the Zulu Empire

and Ancient Carthage,"

added grandpa Kelechi. "The study of history is essential! Knowledge of the past is the foundation on which you build your future."

Chuka nodded. When they arrived at the compound, the delicious smell of yam and pepper soup filled their nostrils. Quickly dropping off their load, they washed up and made their way into the kitchen, where they found grandma Nneka dishing up the food.

"Hello my hard-working, hungry heroes," she said with a cheery chuckle.

"It looks and smells amazing," praised Chuka as he and his grandfather took their places at the dining table.

"Thank you very much for the compliment. That being the case, I'm sure you won't be too upset by the fact that there's no 'grandma's special sauce' today."

"Really? Why not?" asked Chuka, pausing just after he had cut into the soft yam with his tablespoon.

"Because you don't need it anymore," she replied, sitting at the table and preparing to enjoy her meal. "For the seven days you've been here, I have substituted processed sucrose for naturally-occurring fructose-containing fruits. Then I gradually reduced the amounts," she explained, before eating a spoonful of yam, fish and soup. "You didn't even notice. Did you?"

Chuka shook his head.

"Well go on. Try it and see. The proof is in the eating," she smiled.

Chuka ate the piece of yam he had just cut off with his spoon. "Mmm," he masticated, as a contented smile spread across his face.

"Can you taste the natural sugars in the yam?" asked grandpa Kelechi, as he got up to get a second helping.

"Mmm-hmm," replied Chuka, looking up just long enough to answer the question before firmly focusing on filling his face with the fructose and fibrous food.

After lunch, Chuka ventured, as he had for the past few days, to grandpa Kelechi's study to hear his grandfather read from famous books on African history and listen to his advice on health and nutrition.

"Let's see," said his grandfather, looking at the numerous titles in his extensive library. "We've discussed 'When We Ruled' and 'Before The Slave Trade', both by Robin Walker, 'They Came Before Columbus' by Ivan Van Sertima and 'Civilization Or Barbarism' by Cheikh Anta Diop. To be honest, I think that will give you a good understanding of the subject. Perhaps 'Stolen Legacy' by George James."

Grandpa Kelechi started to open the book but then closed it and said. "You know what, I'm going to make a gift of these books to you because they're literally 'must-haves' for anyone who wants to know the story of the Great African continent."

Chuka was quite taken aback by this act of generosity, knowing full well how important these books were to his grandfather. "Wow! Thanks grandad!" he smiled, clasping the books carefully with both hands. "You know, since I began eating more healthily, I've found it much easier to retain all the facts you've taught me over past few days. I wouldn't have been able to remember half of this stuff before. It's brilliant," smiled the appreciative adolescent.

"You're welcome, my boy...*and* you're welcome, my boy," grinned his grandfather.

"You know, as this is your last day and seeing as your parents will be here soon, I'm going to leave you with a final thought on that. Okay?"

Chuka sat up even straighter than he already was.

"The most important thing to understand about processed 'food' is that it's not *actually* food. The definition of food is 'any *nutritious substance* that people or animals eat or drink or that plants absorb in order to maintain life and growth'. A 'nutritious substance' is a food or drink that gives your body the required amount of nutrients (vitamins, minerals, carbohydrates and proteins) to survive. Processed 'food' is *not* nutritious and is *not* required in order to maintain life and growth. Processed 'food' generally acts as a *stimulant*. A stimulant is 'a substance that raises levels of physiological or nervous activity in the body', such as a drug. Just like refined sugar, caffeine, alcohol or nicotine does. Therefore processed 'food' is a *stimulant*, not a food."

Chuka nodded slowly as if in a daze. When he came to, he remarked: "So I guess what you're saying it that processed 'food' should be *treated* as exactly that, a *treat* and *not* as a food."

"You've got it in one, my boy," confirmed grandpa Kelechi.

'Honk-honk!'

The sound of Chuka's parents' car interrupted the 'epiphanial' event. Tutor and tutee exchanged nods before making their way to the front of the house to greet the visitors. Grandma Nneka had already brought them into the parlour and given them something to drink.

"Chuka!" his parents called out, as they hurried to hug their son.

"How are you boy?" asked his dad.

"You look good," mentioned his mum.

"He does look good," agreed his dad.

"You look happy," remarked his mum.

"He does look happy," acknowledged his dad.

Chuka eventually pulled himself away from his parents. "I am happy," he confirmed. "Happy to see you guys, happy to be here, happy in general really."

Chinwe, who had been quiet up until now, came over to her brother and said, "Your face doesn't look half as ashen as it usually does, to be fair."

"Love you too sis," replied Chuka.

"So tell us how this miraculous transformation took place?" enquired Chinwe. You didn't really go into a lot of detail on the phone."

So Chuka told his family the entire story, except for the part about the Arusi of course.

"Well, I still don't *really* know how you guys did it," remarked Chuka's mum to her in-laws. "But we're all *so* happy that you did."

The extended family made their way to the kitchen where grandma Nneka heated up and served the leftover yam and pepper soup, while Chuka's parents explained how they had finally sorted out the problems with their shipping container.

Before long, it was time to leave. Chuka packed his suitcase with the books he had been given by his grandad. Grandma Nneka packed a box full of the fruit and vegetables Chuka had harvested earlier in the day along with healthier versions of her grandson's 'old friends' for the family: baked chin-chin, instead of fried, puff puff, also baked instead of fried and Nigerian coconut candy made using sugar cane juice, pineapple juice and mango juice instead of white sugar. He thanked her for the treats and promised that he'd 'visit' these *new* 'old friends' much more frequently than he did his *old* 'old friends'.

Just before everybody said their goodbyes, grandpa Kelechi decided to make an announcement: "You all know me as a bit of a reserved person, not big on sentiment and such, but seeing the determination to change, that my grandson has shown over these past few days, has encouraged me to do the same." And with that, he walked over and hugged his son, his daughter-in-law, his granddaughter and finally Chuka. The hugs only lasted for a few seconds but were like an age for this retired ship's captain.

"Wow!" exclaimed Chuka's dad, expressing the unspoken sentiment of all the 'hugees'. "Maybe you should visit more often Chuka, if this is the kind of feeling you can inspire."

"I'd like that," replied Chuka, smiling in the direction of his slightly embarrassed grandfather, who smiled and nodded in response.

"Double wow!" exclaimed Chinwe. "You basically had a fit when dad said you'd have to come here!"

Chuka scrunched his eyebrows and shook his head in the direction of his grandparents. "I didn't have a fit."

"Yes you did. Didn't he mum?" countered Chinwe.

"Well -" she began to reply, before grandma Nneka interjected. "It doesn't matter. What is past is past. All we can do is learn from it and use it to guide our actions in the future."

On hearing those sage words, everyone nodded in quiet agreement. Goodbyes finally said, the Akunna family climbed into their car. As he waved to his grandparents, Chuka felt a pang of sadness at the ending of one adventure, but at the same time, a surge of excitement and expectation at the possibility of a new adventure, borne of the first.

Chapter Twelve - A Five A Day Future

"Mr President? Mr. Achebe is here to see you," announced the secretary on the intercom.

"Thank you. Send him in please."

"Chuka! Sorry, 'Mr. President'. How far? Still working out I see," said Chinedu, offering his hand in greeting.

"Chinedu! Looking fresh and lean as always. It goes well my brother," replied Chuka, brushing away the hand of his old friend and giving him a hug. "And how many times have I told you, none of this 'Mr. President' stuff. Okay?" he smiled, gesturing to a chair.

"I know. I'm just playing," chuckled Chinedu. "Who would have thought it? President of Nigeria at just thirty years old," he continued, taking a seat.

"President of *South* Nigeria," corrected Chuka.

"Sorry. *South* Nigeria. Still, what an amazing achievement! And who could forget that speech you gave when you were elected?" Chinedu searched the internet on his phone and pressed play when he found a video of the news story.

"A new dawn for Nigerians. The Nigerian Senate puts into law, former Imo State Governor, now President-elect of South Nigeria, Chuka Akunna's proposal to create three separate countries using the courses of the river Niger and the river Benue as a guide. The countries will be known as North Nigeria, West Nigeria and South Nigeria. The proposal was agreed by a slim majority - nineteen votes to seventeen. During his landmark speech in the senate, President-elect Akunna made the following statement:"

'This 'Frankenstein's monster' of a country should never have existed. It was unnaturally created by people who were not even African and therefore did not understand Africa and African culture...or perhaps they did...This forced together hundreds of different cultures that had existed separately of each other for centuries. We all know the chaos and suffering this has caused our people. The civil war being the worst example of this. But this is a new day! A day for celebration! The borders of our new great nations will not be decided, as it was in the past, by man. The courses of the river Niger and the river Benue were carved, not by man, but by Mother Nature. Mother Africa! And who better to help you make a decision than your mother. My people, we all know about the traditions of our wise Black African ancestors, the Kemetu. As your President, I intend to follow in their ancient footsteps. South Nigerians, I give you my word that all my decisions will be guided by the seven principles and forty-two Ideals of Ma'at. Let us all aspire to this ideal and by doing so, I promise you, we *will* prosper as a nation!'

"The key components of the directive are as follows: South Nigeria's boundaries will be based on the so-called 'Eastern Region' of Nigeria in 1960 and will revert to a three state country: Cross River State, East Central State and Rivers State based on the 1967 map of Nigeria. The boundaries of West Nigeria and North Nigeria will also adhere to the 1960 configuration of the former country. Each new country will have its own independent government, central bank, currency and flag. The revenue from the oil reserves of the south will be managed by a firm jointly owned by all three countries and shared equally between them. Freedom of movement of peoples across the three countries will be permitted, as long as individuals abide by the sovereign law of the nation they travel to."

"I still get goose bumps!" declared Chinedu, pausing the video. "I remember the packed streets, the deafening car horns, the banners sporting your name, the endless cheers of the youth when news of your election to office was announced. It was an even bigger reaction than when you were elected as Imo State Governor six years ago."

Chuka sighed. "Yes. It has been an incredible time in my life and the life of all Nigerians-North, South and West. And here we are today, three years after my election as President, on the cusp of another great adventure."

Chinedu leant back in his chair. "Well, if the last six years are anything to go by, I think you'll manage just fine because all the policies you introduced over the years have always been pragmatic and popular. It was only after you got elected as Imo State Governor and passed the 'Promote Local Innovation Bill' that 'Imolites' like me could secure grants to grow our businesses."

"Yeah but *you* were the one who came up with so many ingenious ways to sustainably grow and use palm fruit, palm kernels, palm kernel shells, palm oil, palm nut oil, palm wine, palm fronds...Did I miss anything?" smiled Chuka.

"No, I think you just about covered it," replied Chinedu, with a grin.

"And it was innovators like *you* who used that grant wisely and raised further funds locally so you could manufacture refined palm products and sell them all over the globe." Chuka paused and then smiled before saying: "You could say that you've got the world in the *palm* of your hands. Mmm? Mmm?"

Chinedu laughed and shook his head. "You really need some new material, bro."

"Seriously though, like I've always said, you're like a modern day George Washington Carver," said

Chuka, leaning forward with his hands across his desk.

Chinedu nodded. "Well thanks to your programme, this new country of ours has modern day versions of:

Lewis Latimer, who in 1881, invented the light bulb carbon filament,

Jesse E. Russell, who invented the digital cellular base station that paved the way for modern cell-phones,

George R. Carruthers, who invented the ultraviolet camera/spectrograph for NASA's Apollo 16 rocket,

Creola K. Johnson, whose mathematical calculations were critical to the success of NASA spaceflights,

Gladys Mae West, whose mathematical equations were vital for GPS and therefore SatNavs,

James Edward West, who invented the microphone most widely used in the world today,

Granville T. Woods, who in 1885, invented a telephone/telegraph for the railways in the U.S,

Valerie L. Thomas, who invented the '3D Illusion Transmitter', which produces 3D projections of objects,

Percy Lavon Julian, who invented synthetic cortisone, for use in extreme pain relief,

Gerald A. Lawson, who, in 1976, invented the first video game system with swappable cartridges,

Frederick M. Jones, who invented 'mobile refrigeration', in the form of the refrigerated truck,

Dr. Shirley Ann Jackson, whose pioneering research lead to touch-tone phones, caller ID and call-waiting,

Marie Van Brittan Brown, who, in 1966, invented the home security system,

Otis Boykin, who invented an electrical control unit for the artificial heart pacemaker,

Dr. Charles Drew, who invented the modern blood bank, that saved thousands of Allied lives in WWII,

Marian R. Croak, who invented VoIP protocol, which allowed calls to be made over the internet,

Lloyd A. Hall, who invented ways to preserve food, sterilize medicine, medical instruments and cosmetics,

Garrett Morgan, who invented the gas mask and the three-light Traffic Light,

Thomas L. Jennings, who, in 1821, invented dry-cleaning,

Dr. Mark E. Dean, who invented the IBM Personal Computer,

Dr. Patricia Bath, who invented a device that refined laser cataract surgery,

Lonnie G. Johnson, who invented the 'Super Soaker'

and of course, George Washington Carver, who invented 300 products made from peanuts."

"That's pretty amazing stuff, but why do you have that list of famous Black African inventors with you?" asked an inquisitive and intrigued Chuka.

"This?" said Chinedu, putting the piece of paper back in his shirt pocket. "Well I've been asked to put something together about the rich history of Black African inventors and their incredible contributions to the world, for the primary schools, secondary schools and universities of South Nigeria to help encourage the youth of this country to follow in their footsteps."

"Just like you did."

"Precisely," replied Chinedu.

Chuka's mobile phone 'pinged', interrupting them. Taking a look at the screen, he smiled broadly, pressed the intercom for his secretary and said: "Chiamaka, my parents are coming up. Please show them in when they arrive."

"Yes sir."

"It'll be nice to see your mum and dad again," remarked Chinedu, pouring himself a glass of chilled water and looking through the glass partition at the bustling East Central State office.

When Chuka's parents arrived, Chinedu greeted them respectfully by standing up and shaking their hands. "Good morning Mr and Mrs Akunna," he said, vacating the chair he was sitting on for Chuka's dad and bringing another one from a corner of the room for his mum. Chuka also rose from his chair and walked over to embrace his parents.

"Hi mum. Hi dad. How was the drive over?" he asked, gesturing to them to sit.

"It was very smooth, from start to finish, my son. The infrastructure projects you put in place over the past few years have really made road travel a breeze," replied his dad.

"Would you guys like something to drink?"

"Just some cold water please, my child. This May weather is really something else," remarked Chuka's mum, looking to her husband for confirmation, who nodded in reply to both her comments.

"I'll get it," said Chinedu, gesturing to Chuka with a raised palm. "Thank goodness for air-conditioning," he remarked, enjoying the cool breeze as he poured the drinks for Chuka's parents. "This, incidentally," he continued, "is something millions of South Nigerians can say nowadays, thanks to your 'Solar Power-Powers People' initiative.

"We remember the bad old days of 'NEPA'. Don't we darling?" remarked Chuka's dad.

"Indeed we do," grimaced his wife. "Thankfully, nowadays, a regular supply of electricity is the norm and not the exception. Your support for the solar energy companies has given, even the smallest of villages, access to an uninterrupted electricity supply."

"Ah ah, my dear," chimed in her husband. "You didn't even mention his most important initiative. The one that got him elected."

"The 'Equal Share' policy!" all three of them said together.

"The law that guarantees every citizen of South Nigeria, receives an equal share of the oil revenues generated by the country. It was such a ground-breaking policy and at the same time such an obvious one," commented Chinedu, handing Chuka's parents their drinks.

"Affectionately known as the 'Everyone Qualifies Under Akunna's Law,' " smiled Chuka's mum. "And they all did," she concluded.

"We all do," added his dad. "You should be very proud of yourself son. I know *we* all are."

"Thank you guys, but it's definitely not been a 'one man show' though. The state governors of our new nation have been incredibly supportive of the plans I put forward and have been very open-minded about how we achieve them."

A mobile phone rang. Everyone pulled their phones out of their pockets and bags, but in the end

Chuka's dad won this round of 'whose phone is it this time?'

"Hello my darling. Yes, we're already here. Okay, I'll tell him." Putting his phone back in his pocket, he said to his son: "That was your sister. She's down at reception."

"Okay," replied Chuka, pressing the button on his intercom. "Chiamaka. My sister's in reception. Send her up please."

"Yes sir," she replied.

Chinwe was on her phone as she entered the office. "That's not going to work for me. Can you call me back when they've tabled a better offer? Thanks. Bye. Hello everyone!" she announced, putting her phone away and hugging everyone.

"Chinedu. Long time. How far?" she asked of her old friend.

"I am well 'my sister'. How's your hubby and kids?" he enquired, pulling up another chair for her.

"They are well 'my brother'. Eze is working from home today so he's looking after the children. I'm not sure how much work he is getting done though," she smiled, as she took out a bottle of mineral water from her bag and took a sip.

Now hugging Chuka, she said: "Hey there little bro'. How're you feeling?"

"I'm good sis. Good to see you," responded Chuka, mid embrace.

"Hey Chuka, do you remember when you first got elected and I said to you: 'I guess I can't really say 'you're not the boss of me' anymore?' Because technically you *were* the boss of me and everyone else in the country for that matter," laughed Chinwe.

"Oh yeah. I remember," chuckled Chuka.

"It all seems so long ago now," reminisced Chinwe, finally taking a seat.

"What seems so long ago is the twenty years that have passed since that fateful visit to see his grandparents. I still can hardly believe how quickly he adopted a healthy lifestyle, including eating plenty of fruits, vegetables and nuts - something I thought I'd *never* see," proclaimed Chuka's dad.

"It's true," added his mum. "Gone were the days of him eating loads of sugary snacks and processed food. They were all replaced by healthy home-made meals. Cooked 'from scratch', by yours truly, I might add."

"I remember you guys taking him to see our family doctor," remarked Chinwe, joining the family walk down memory lane. "What was his name? Anunuso? That was it. Dr. Anunuso. He referred him to a nutritionist who advised him on how to eat a balanced diet and on the benefits of regular exercise."

"Yeah, it was difficult at first but after a while it just became the norm," recalled Chuka.

"I recollect a particularly complimentary editorial about your life growing up," chimed in Chinedu, scrolling through the internet on his mobile phone again.

"Ah, here it is. It's kind of long, so I'll just read the last paragraph. 'Soon Chuka was no longer 'just a boy in the middle'. Now he was the boy at the top. Top of his class, top of his year, top scorer in his football team, top marks in his exams. And all this because, without the excess sugar 'clouding his brain,' he could effectively retain, analyse, interpret and reproduce what he learnt in school. He was no longer greedy for cakes, sweets or candy. Now he gorged himself on maths, science and history. Now he feasted on knowledge.' "

After a pregnant pause, Chinwe asked: "Weren't you going out with that reporter? What was her name?"

"Ijeoma," answered Chuka and Chinedu together with broad smiles.

"Anyway," said Chuka, getting up from his chair and walking up to his sister. "That's enough about me. What's new with you sis? How's business?"

Chinwe quickly checked her phone before replying. "You'll be happy to know that the family business is doing very well. Thanks to your policies supporting manufacturers of refined goods like Chinedu here, we have changed from an import-export firm to more of an export-export firm. Your government's policy of not accepting foreign government loans or handouts and instead funding innovation from existing internal country revenues, plus offering citizens' incentives to buy shares in local and national companies, has also helped us grow the business at an incredible rate. The people have a real stake in their country, so they put in a real effort to contribute to its success."

Chuka's mobile phone rudely interrupted his sister's speech. The reason it rang, however, was much more pleasant. "Hi grandpa. Yeah, yeah. Chinedu will come down to collect you," he said, motioning the request to Chinedu with his eyes. "Okay. See you in a minute."

Chinedu made his way to the door.

"Thanks bro," said Chuka.

"It looks like everyone will be here for the big moment," smiled Chinwe.

"Looks that way," said Chuka. "I hardly get to see you guys these days. We're all so busy. So it's really nice that we can all get together. Especially on a day like this. You know?"

"Igbo kwenu!" shouted grandpa Kelechi as he entered the office, to which everyone replied, "Hey!"

"Igbo kwenu!" he called again.

Again, the room replied: "Hey!"

"Kwezue nu!"

"Heyyy!"

After all the embraces and greetings were complete, grandma Nneka handed Chuka a red, black, green and gold striped enamel bowl with a matching lid.

"What's this?" he asked.

"It's just a little freshly roasted yam, plantain and spicy tomato sauce to help you keep up your strength," she replied.

"Ah ah. Thank you, ma," said Chuka, embracing her a second time.

Chuka's parents vacated the two chairs directly in front of his desk, so that grandma Nneka and grandpa Kelechi could take centre stage. Immediately, he brought them water to drink.

"It really makes an old man proud to see his family and his people doing so well," said grandpa Kelechi, looking around the room.

"These are indeed happy times grandfather," responded Chuka, perching himself on the edge of his desk directly in front of his grandparents. "It is, however, important to note that in our new country, we are South Nigerians *first* and Igbo *second*. The destructive tribalism of the old Nigeria cannot and will not be part of our new nation."

"You speak well young man. And of course, you are correct. You have always been a true statesman. Someone who actually cares for his country and the people. In complete contrast to those career politicians who care for nothing but themselves," responded the nonagenarian.

"Steady on grandpa," smiled Chinwe, placing her hand on his shoulder. "This is the same guy who sneaked a shopping bag full of sweets, cakes and biscuits into your house. Remember? He's hardly perfect," she chuckled.

"We all remember that. Don't we?" remarked grandpa Kelechi with a grin, looking around the room at the smiling and nodding faces. "That childish interlude aside, I truly believe that, with people like Chuka at the helm, in time, our new country will be likened to the Great African nations of old."

"High praise indeed grandfather. It would be a great honour to be in such illustrious company," remarked Chuka. "Hopefully over time, we will reach those historic heights. We are also hoping to emulate modern African national success stories like Botswana, Rwanda and Ghana...."

'Knock-knock'.

"Pardon the interruption sir," said Chuka's secretary, poking her head round the door. "The results are coming through."

The extended Akunna family and Chinedu followed her into the outer office and joined the President's administrative team, as they turned on the flat-screen TV in the middle of the room and gathered round it.

"The odds-on favourite, Chuka Akunna, remains well ahead in the race," commented the news presenter. "I'm here in Addis Ababa with political commentator, Tunde Ade as we try to analyse the reasons for his runaway lead."

"Thank you, Funke. The reasons for this are quite straightforward, if you think about it. Look at what President Akunna has already done for the 'recently born' country of South Nigeria. The country's natural resources now directly benefit the masses rather than a select few at the top. This has been provided to the people in the form of lower taxes, free healthcare and free education. The formation of a robust legislative and judicial system means that rich and poor alike can expect to be treated fairly under the law. He has married capitalism with socialism in a way that brings out the best of the two systems, allowing the economy to grow without exploiting the people or the environment. Low tariffs on imports combined with business friendly internal policies, like subsidising farmers, has greatly boosted the agricultural and manufacturing sectors. This has all led to a very prosperous country. Speaking personally, as a citizen of West Nigeria, I hope that my President, Funlola Adeboya is taking note."

"So do I Tunde. Now from what I understand, his ideas are not reserved for South Nigeria alone, but for the continent of Africa as a whole. What can you tell us about that?"

"Well Funke, again we see similar forward-thinking ideas, such the creation of an African Central Bank, owned and run exclusively by African nations, that use the vast wealth already within the continent to fund infrastructure projects rather than relying on unnecessary and often exorbitant foreign loans. The creation of a continental 'trading-bloc' so that the *entire continent of Africa* sits at the 'negotiating table', rather than small nations like Djibouti. The formation of a Pan-African defence system to protect our borders. The teaching of an Afro-centric curriculum in schools, especially with regards to history. Finally, his 'One Africa-One Language' ('Moja Afrika-Lugha Moja') policy, to make Kiswahili - the most spoken language on the continent - the official language of the African people. In his words, 'to bring the Motherland together, under the same mother tongue'. The speech he gave at the African Union last year, I believe, sums it up quite well. And I quote: 'A common spoken language will promote smoother and more efficient inter-country interaction and collaboration and, perhaps even more importantly, aid continental unity by signifying a significant and essential break from the use of invasive foreign languages that resulted in an alien culture being forced upon the continent of Africa'."

Everyone was so taken by the tale being transmitted on the television that no one, not even grandpa Kelechi, noticed that his wife had silently slipped away from the expectant crowd for a brief moment. Grandma Nneka returned from Chuka's office, with her home-made roasted yam, plantain and spicy tomato sauce, which she had warmed up in the microwave. After several 'pardon me's' and a few 'excuse me's', she finally found her way back to his position in the middle of the crowd.

"Chuka my boy, you forgot this. You need to keep your strength up. Remember?" she said quietly, handing the enamel bowl to him, along with a fork she had borrowed from the office kitchen.

"I remember. Thank you, grandma," he replied, smiling down at her.

The TV presenters and political commentators continued their analysis of the election as Chuka enjoyed the sweet, smoky and spicy flavours of the food. Halfway through eating, what was quite a large portion of food, the moment of truth arrived.

"Hold that thought Tunde," said the Reporter, holding her earpiece firmly. "I believe we have a confirmed result coming through. "Yes. It's official. The first democratically elected President of the continent of Africa is Chuka Akunna, the current President of South Nigeria!"

Expecting everyone to celebrate the incredible news by yelling, jumping on him, chest-bumping him or vigorously patting his back, Chuka quickly put the bowl down on a table, closed his eyes and braced himself for the imminent impact and the cacophony of noise.

Nothing.

He opened his eyes to find all the people paused in their own particular pouncing positions.

The image before him, Chuka imagined, was like watching a video of the team-mates of a football player, who had just scored the winning penalty in the World Cup Final, and then pausing it *just* as the ball hits the back of the net.

Even though it had been some twenty years since the last time, he instantly recognised her handiwork. "Frankie?!" he yelled, carefully manoeuvring himself out from the middle of the crowd.

"You called, my main melanated man?" she replied, appearing in front of him.

"Don't *do* that!" cried the startled statesman.

When his heart had returned to its regular rhythm, he asked, "Where's your 'partner in *time*'?"

"Partner in time? Oh, yeah, yeah, right. Good one Mr. President," said Frankie, rolling her eyes.

"Hang on, I've got another one. And you'd be Zabrina's 'partner in *thyme*'. Get it. Like the herb. Because you're made from vegetables."

"Really Chuka? You just won the greatest electoral victory of your life. You're three for three in fact. And you're making jokes…Anyway, he isn't my partner. He's definitely his own Arusi and he was only with me because you 'summoned' him. Remember?"

"Him?" questioned Chuka. "I thought Zabrina was a 'her'."

"He was a 'her'. Now he's back to being a 'he'…it's complicated," advised Frankie.

"I'm sure it is. Anyway, why are you here? You're not here to tell me that this is some kind of illusion, are you? Or that all this happened because of some magic spell?"

Frankie smiled. "Oh no. This is definitely real and it's not the result of some magic trick either…Although it could have been."

"What do you mean by that?"

"It's not a big deal really."

"Come on. Out with it."

"Well...you remember back in your bedroom at your grandparents' house, when you said that you preferred your grandmother's biscuits to the shop-bought ones?"

"Y-e-a-h."

"Okay, I kind of made a bet with Zabrina that if you chose your grandma's biscuits over your favourite shop-bought ones, that she would basically grant you three wishes. And if you chose the shop-bought ones...you and I…would never have met..." Her voice trailed off.

Chuka stared at Frankie for a moment. "So you're saying that you guys wagered the direction of my entire life on the taste of a baked good? We mortals are just playthings to you demi-gods, aren't we?"

"Action-figures to be specific," quipped Frankie. "You know, because your arms and legs are poseable."

Chuka glared his response.

"Listen, Chuka. After all we'd been through together; I absolutely, positively knew that you'd choose your grandmother's biscuits. And on the flip side, if you *had* chosen the shop-bought ones, then there was really no hope for you and you wouldn't have wanted to meet me anyway...Did I mention the three wishes?"

Chuka stared at Frankie again. "Fine. Tell me more about the wishes. Not that I want to use them right now, but I have a feeling that one day I, or rather the continent, may need them."

"Okay, so technically, they're not wishes like the genie wishes you've seen in movies. These are based on Zabrina's demi-god powers over bargaining, chaos and change. She can help you control these elements of human behaviour, if the need ever arises," explained Frankie.

"...Okay...thanks...I imagine they may come in quite handy one day."

Feeling a little overwhelmed, Chuka sat down and looked up at the TV, which had the words: 'Chuka Akunna - President of Africa' etched across it. Still staring at the screen, he pondered out loud. "Are we really saying that eating my five-a-day lead to *all of this*? Are we *really* saying that?"

"I'm saying that it definitely played an important part in your achievements," replied Frankie. "Take for example you joining the debate team at university. The old you, would never have had the confidence to stand up in front of a hundred people and proceed to persuade them of the merits of following the ancient Kemetic teachings of Ma'at - in the first year of your African History degree no less." Frankie continued with her point. "Did a healthy balanced diet and regular exercise, magically make you the President of Africa? No, of course not. Did it play a significant part in achieving it? *Absolutely*. Because it was the foundation of your success. Without that foundation, you wouldn't have had the physical or mental strength necessary, for the hard work and discipline that was required to create your success."

"So I guess what you're saying is that my five-a-day foundation was the fulcrum that helped me forge this fantastic future," said Chuka, making his back to his original position in the middle of the static crowd and taking his seat.

"I couldn't have put it better myself," replied Frankie.

"Okay Frankie, now I'm ready to forge *Africa's* future."

For the final time, Frankie raised her fruity fingers. "Alright, but once I wave my hand, that future begins. Are you sure you're ready?"

"Yes, I am," replied Chuka, bracing himself for the impending people pile-up.

Just then, he noticed the unfinished bowl of roasted fruit and vegetables his grandma had given him, resting on the desk beside him.

"Actually, hang on. Just let me finish this yam and plantain..."

Acknowledgments

Many thanks to Jana, Adanna and Obinne
for your advice and support.

Printed in Great Britain
by Amazon